THE CARPENTER'S PENCIL

Manuel Rivas

THE CARPENTER'S PENCIL

Translated from the Galician by
Jonathan Dunne

THE OVERLOOK PRESS
WOODSTOCK & NEW YORK

First published in the United States in 2001 by
The Overlook Press, Peter Mayer Publishers, Inc.
Woodstock & New York

WOODSTOCK:
One Overlook Drive
Woodstock, NY 12498
www.overlookpress.com
[for individual orders, bulk and special sales, contact our Woodstock office]

NEW YORK:
386 West Broadway
New York, NY 10012

This edition has been translated with the financial assistance of the
Spanish Dirección General del Libro y Bibliotecas, Ministerio de Cultura

First published in Galician by Edicións Xerais de Galicia in 1998 as *O lapis do carpinteiro*,
and by Editorial Alfaguara in a Spanish translation by Dolores Vilavedra,
with the title *El lápiz del carpintero*, in 1998

Library of Congress Cataloging-in-Publication Data

Rivas, Manuel.
[Lapis do carpinteiro. English]
The carpenter's pencil / Manuel Rivas.
p. cm.
I. Title
PGQ9469.2.R5 L3713 2001   869.3'421—dc21   2001021101
Manufactured in the United States of America
FIRST EDITION
1 3 5 7 9 8 6 4 2
ISBN 1-58567-145-2

TRANSLATOR'S NOTE

The Carpenter's Pencil is already the most widely-translated work in the history of Galician literature. Very few other works of Galician literature have been translated into English: Cunqueiro's Merlin and Company, Murado's A Bestiary of Discontent, an anthology of Galician short stories, of Méndez Ferrín's short stories, of Rosalía de Castro's poetry.

We have taken the unusual step of including two poems at the end of the book, with the author's approval. The first is Rosalía de Castro's poem "Justice by the Hand", referred to in chapter 6. Rosalía is Galicia's most revered writer. The second is described in chapter 19 as "the best poem of humanity". It seemed unfair to leave such an assertion hanging in the air without clarification. Whether or not the reader agrees, of course, is quite another matter.

The translator expresses his heartfelt gratitude to The Tyrone Guthrie Centre in Ireland, where he translated part of this novel, to Graham Watt and Doctor Edward Coomes, and to the author, Manuel Rivas, for his help at all times.

To Chonchiña, and in memory of her great love, Paco Comesaña,
Doctor Comesaña, healer of melancholy.
To Ánxel Vázquez de la Cruz, paediatrician at Coruña
Maternity and Children's Hospital.
Without them this story would not have come into being.

In memory also of Camilo Díaz Baliño, painter murdered on 14 August 1936,
and Xerardo Díaz Fernández, author of Os que non morreron
("Those who did not die")
and A crueldade inútil ("Pointless cruelty"), who died in exile in Montevideo.

With my gratitude to Doctors Héctor Verea, who guided me
in the matter of tuberculosis,
and Domingo García-Sabell, who acquainted me with the
beguiling figure of Roberto Nóvoa Santos,
professor of general pathology, who died in 1933.

I was also helped a great deal by reference to the historical research of
Dionisio Pereira, V. Luis Lamela and Carlos Fernández.

To Juan Cruz, who said quite simply, "Why don't you write this story?"
and gave Rosa López a pretty carpenter's pencil from China to give to me.

To Quico Cadaval and Xurxo Souto, who breathe stories and the light of mists.
To Xosé Luís de Dios, who with his painting reminded me of the washerwomen.

And to Isa, on the crags of Pasarela,
among the apiaries of Cova de Ladróns.

1

"HE'S UPSTAIRS, ON THE BALCONY, LISTENING TO the blackbirds."

Carlos Sousa, the journalist, said thank you when she invited him in with the gesture of a smile. "Yes, thank you," he thought as he went up the stairs, "there should be two eyes like those at every front door."

Doctor Da Barca was sitting in a wicker chair, a small brazier under the table next to him, his hand resting on an open book, as if pressing and pondering on a brilliant page. He was looking out over the garden, which was shrouded in winter light. The scene would have been a peaceful one had it not been for the oxygen mask he was using to breathe. The tube linking him to the cylinder was draped over the white azalea flowers. Sousa found the image disturbingly and comically sad.

Doctor Da Barca, realizing he had a visit on account of the creaking floorboards, stood up and put the mask to one side with surprising agility, like the control of a child's console. He was tall and broad-shouldered, and held up his arms in a gesture of greeting. He seemed made for the act of embracing.

Sousa felt confused. He was expecting someone on their death-bed and was ill at ease with the task of drawing the last words from an old man whose life had been eventful. He thought the voice would be thin and incoherent, locked in a pathetic struggle against Alzheimer's disease. He never could have imagined such a luminous demise, as if in reality the patient were connected up to a generator. This was not his disease, but Doctor Da Barca had the consumptive beauty of those suffering from tuberculosis. His eyes wide like lamps veiled in blue. Pale as pottery, a pink varnish on his cheeks.

"Your reporter's here," she said, still smiling. "Isn't he young?"

"Not that young," Sousa replied with a modest look in her direction. "I'm not the man I used to be."

"Sit down, sit down," said Doctor Da Barca. "I was just trying the oxygen. Would you like some?"

The reporter Sousa felt partially relieved. This beautiful, ageing woman who had come to the door, seemingly chosen on a whim by the chisel of Time. This very sick man, out of hospital two days previously, with the spirit of a cycling champion. It had been suggested to him at the news-paper, "Why don't you give him an interview? He's an old exile. Apparently he even had dealings with Che Guevara in Mexico."

Who was interested in that nowadays? Only a head of local news who read *Le Monde Diplomatique* at night. Sousa detested politics. To tell the truth, he detested journalism. He had recently been working in Accident and Crime. It had got too much for him. The world was a dung-heap.

Doctor Da Barca's elongated fingers flapped like keys of their own volition, as if attached to the organ out of age-old loyalty. The reporter Sousa felt those fingers were exploring him, percussing his body. He had the suspicion the doctor was observing him, analysing the meaning of the bags under his eyes, his prematurely puffed-up eyelids, as if he were sick.

"I could well be," he thought.

"Marisa, love, bring us something to drink. We don't want to spoil the obituary."

"The things you come out with!" she exclaimed. "You shouldn't joke like that."

The reporter Sousa was about to decline but realized that turning down a drink would be a mistake. His body had been asking for one for hours – drink, blasted drink – ever since he had got out of bed, and it was at that moment he knew he was dealing with one of those sorcerers who can read others' minds.

"I don't suppose you're an H-Two-O man?"

"No," he said, continuing with the irony, "my problem is not exactly water."

"Wonderful. We've a Mexican tequila that brings back the dead. Two glasses, Marisa, if you please." He then winked in his direction, "My grandchildren do not forget their revolutionary grandfather."

"How are you feeling?" Sousa asked. He had to start somehow.

"As you can see," said the doctor, jovially spreading his arms, "I'm dying. Do you really think an interview with me holds any interest?"

The reporter Sousa recalled what he had been told over drinks at the Café Oeste. Doctor Da Barca was an old and uncompromising Republican, who had been condemned to death in 1936 and had saved his skin by a miracle. "By a miracle," one of the informants had concurred. After his prison sentence, he had gone into exile in Mexico, from where he had returned to the ancestral home only on the death of Franco. He still had his ideas. Or the Idea, as he used to say. "A man of another time," the informant had called him.

"I am what you would call an ectoplasm," the doctor told him. "Or an alien if you prefer. That is why I have trouble breathing."

The head of local news had given him a cutting from the paper with a photograph and a short notice about a public homage to the doctor. People were grateful for the way he cared for the humblest among them and never charged. "His front door's not been locked since the day of his return from exile," said one woman living next door. Sousa explained he was sorry not to have visited him sooner, the interview was meant for before his admission to hospital.

"You're not from here, are you, Sousa?" said the doctor,

switching the conversation away from himself.

He replied that he wasn't, that he came from further north. He had only been there for a couple of years and what he liked most was the clemency of the weather, which was tropical for Galicia. Occasionally he would go to Portugal and eat *bacalao* à la Gomes de Sáa.

"Forgive my curiosity, but do you live alone?"

The reporter Sousa looked around for the woman, but she had slipped away quietly, leaving the glasses and the bottle of tequila. It was a strange situation, the interviewer being interviewed. He was going to say he did, he lived very alone, far too alone, but he responded by laughing. "I've got my landlady, she worries terribly that I'm growing thin. She's a Portuguese, married to a Galician. When they argue, she calls her husband a Portuguese and he says she's just like a Galician. That's without the adjectives, of course. They're a bit strong."

Doctor Da Barca smiled thoughtfully. Then he said, "The only good thing about borders are the secret crossings. It's incredible the effect an imaginary line can have. It gets traced one day by some doddering king in his bed or drawn on the table by powerful men as if they were playing a game of poker. I remember a terrible thing a man once said to me, 'My grandfather was the lowest of the low.' 'Why? What did he do?' I asked. 'Did he kill someone?' 'No, no. My paternal grandfather served a Portuguese.' He was drunk with historical bile. 'Well,' I said to annoy him, 'if I were to choose a passport, I'd be a Portuguese.' Fortunately, however, this border will soon be swallowed up in its own absurdity. True borders are those that keep the poor away from a share of the cake."

Doctor Da Barca moistened his lips on the glass and then raised it in a toast. "You know? I am a revolutionary," he said suddenly, "an internationalist. Of the kind that existed before. Of the kind who belonged to the First International, I would have to confess. Now, I bet that sounds strange to you."

"I'm not interested in politics," Sousa replied instinctively. "I'm interested in the person."

"In the person, yes," murmured Da Barca. "Have you heard of Doctor Nóvoa Santos?"

"No."

"He was a very interesting person. He expounded the theory of intelligent reality."

"I'm afraid I do not know him."

"That's nothing to be ashamed of. Hardly anyone remembers him, beginning with the majority of doctors. Intelligent reality, that was it. We all let out a thread, like silkworms. We gnaw at and fight over the white mulberry leaves, but that thread, if it crosses over with others and intertwines, can make a beautiful fabric, an unforgettable cloth."

It was getting late. A blackbird flew in a pentagram out of the orchard as if in haste to make a forgotten rendezvous on the other side of the border. The beautiful, ageing woman approached the balcony again with the gentle flow of a water-clock.

"Marisa," he said all of a sudden, "what was that poem about the blackbird, the one poor Faustino wrote?"

So much passion and so much melody
Was squeezed into your veins,
Add another passion, your body
Is so frail it would break.

He recited it uncoaxed and unaffected, as if in response to a natural request. What moved the reporter Sousa was his expression, a glow of stained-glass windows in the twilight. He took a swig of the tequila to see how much it burned.

"What do you think?"

"Very beautiful," Sousa said. "Who's it by?"

"A priest who was a poet and was very fond of women." He smiled, "A case of intelligent reality."

"So how did you two meet?" the reporter asked, ready at last to take notes.

"I had noticed him walking in the Alameda. But the first time I heard him speak was in a theatre," explained Marisa, her eyes on the doctor. "Some girl friends had taken me. It was a Republican event to debate whether or not women should have the right to vote. Now it seems strange, but in those days there was a lot of controversy, even among women. Isn't that so? And then Daniel stood up and told the story about the queen of the bees . . . Do you remember, Daniel?"

"What's the story about the queen of the bees?" Sousa asked, intrigued.

"In antiquity no-one knew where bees came from. Wise men such as Aristotle invented outlandish theories. It was said, for example, that bees emerged from the stomach of dead oxen. This carried on for centuries. And do you know why it carried on for so long? Because no-one had the courage to see that the king was a queen. How can freedom be maintained on the basis of such a lie?"

"The clapping went on for ages," Marisa added.

"Well, it was not an indescribable ovation," remarked the doctor humorously. "But yes, there was some applause."

Marisa continued,

"I liked him. But after hearing him that day I began to like him a lot. Even more so when my family warned me off him, 'You should have nothing to do with that man.' They soon found out who he was."

"I thought she was a seamstress."

Marisa laughed,

"Yes, I lied to him. I went to get a dress made at a tailor's opposite his mother's house. I came out of the fitting and he was on his way back from visiting patients. He looked at me, carried on walking, and suddenly turned around, 'Do you work here?' I nodded. 'Well, you're the prettiest seamstress I know. You must sew with silk.'"

Doctor Da Barca looked at her, his old eyes tattooed with desire.

"Somewhere amongst the archaeological ruins of Santiago, there must still be a rusty revolver, the one she brought us in prison in an attempt to save us."

2

HERBAL HARDLY EVER SPOKE.

He would wipe down the tables, meticulously, like someone buffing an instrument. He would empty the ashtrays. He would sweep the floor, very slowly, allowing the broom time to rummage in the corners. He would use a spray whose fragrance was Canadian pine, so it said on the can, and it was he who lit the neon sign by the roadside, with its red lettering and Valkyrian figure who seemed to be lifting her tits like weights with her brawny biceps. He would plug in the stereo and play that album, *Ciao, amore*, which would continue all night long like a litany of the flesh. Manila would clap her hands, do up her hair as if about to perform in a cabaret for the first time, and then Herbal would unbolt the door.

Manila would say,

"Come on, girls. It's the white shoes today."

White tuna. Fishmeal. Cocaine. The white shoes had taken over the territory of the old smugglers from Fronteira.

Herbal would remain with his elbows on the end of the bar,

like a sentry in his box. They knew he was there, filming every movement, scrutinizing the ones who, he used to say, had silver faces and razor-tongues. Only occasionally would he leave his lookout post to help Manila with the drinks, at the rare times it got busy, and he would do so in the manner of a barman at the height of war, as if he were pouring the spirits straight into the client's liver.

Maria da Visitação had arrived not long before from an island off the African Atlantic coast. Without any official documents. She had been sold to Manila, so to speak. Of her new country she had seen little more than the road that went to Fronteira. She would look at it from the window of the flat, in the same building as the club, which was set on its own, away from neighbouring houses. In the window was a geranium. If we could see her from the outside, as she watched motionless at the window, we would think red butterflies had landed on the beautiful totem of her face.

On the other side of the road, there was a chestnut grove with mimosas. They had helped her a great deal that first winter. They flowered like candles on a roadside altar, and that vision kept her from feeling cold. That and the blackbirds' singing, the melancholy whistling of black souls. Behind the grove was a dump for cars. Sometimes people could be seen searching through the scrap for spares. But the only full-time resident was a dog chained to a car without wheels that served as its kennel. It would climb up on to the roof and bark all day. This made her feel cold. She thought that she was very far north; that from Fronteira upwards was a world of mists, gales and snow. The men that descended bore lighthouses in their eyes, rubbed their hands together on entering the club and drank strong liquor.

With a few exceptions, they spoke very little.

Like Herbal.

She got on well with Herbal. He had never threatened her nor raised his hand to strike her, as she had heard happened to the girls at other clubs on the road. Manila had not hit her either, though there were days her mouth resembled the barrel of a sawn-off shotgun. Maria da Visitação had realized that food dictated her mood. When she inclined to eating, she would treat them like daughters. But the days she thought she had put on weight, she would spit out blasphemies as if in an attempt to spew out the fat. None of the girls was sure what kind of relationship existed between Herbal and Manila. They slept together. Or at least they slept in the same room. In the club they behaved like proprietress and employee, but without giving or receiving orders. She never blasphemed when she was talking to him.

The club opened at nightfall and they slept in the day. It was early in the afternoon when Maria da Visitação came downstairs. She had woken with a hangover, her mouth like an ashtray, her vagina sore from the traffickers' strenuous thrusts, and she felt like mixing a lemon juice with cold beer. Seated at a table under a lamp that opened a pool of light in the semi-darkness, with the shutters closed, was Herbal.

He was drawing on paper napkins with a carpenter's pencil.

3

"'I'M SORRY, PAL.' AND MY UNCLE WOULD SQUEEZE the trigger. 'I wish I didn't have to, my friend.' And then my uncle would hit hard with the stick, a well-aimed blow to the back of the fox's neck as it lay caught in the trap. A look would flash between my uncle, the trapper, and his prey. His eyes would be saying, and I heard the murmur, that there was nothing he could do. This is what I felt before the painter. I did a lot of bad things, but when I was with the painter, I murmured to myself that I was sorry, that I wished I didn't have to, and I don't know what he thought when our eyes met, a moist blaze in the night, but I want to believe that he understood, that he saw that I was doing it to save him torment. Without further ado, without moving from where I was, I put the pistol to his temple and blew off his head. And then I remembered the pencil. The pencil he carried behind his ear. This pencil."

4

THE MEMBERS OF THE PARTY, THE ESCORTS WHO called themselves the Dawn Brigade, were fuming. First of all they looked at him in surprise, as if to say, "What an idiot, he didn't mean to shoot, that's not how you kill." But then, on the way back, they kept thinking that his diligence had spoiled their fun. They had envisaged something really evil. Perhaps cutting off his balls while he was still alive and stuffing them into his mouth. Or cutting off his hands as they did to the painter Francisco Miguel or the tailor Luís Huici. Try sewing now, dandy!

"Don't upset yourself, girl, these are the sort of things that happened," Herbal said to Maria da Visitação. "I know of one who went to offer a widow his condolences and left a finger of her husband's in her hand. She knew it was his on account of the wedding ring."

The prison governor, a tormented man and, rumour had it, an old friend of some of those inside, had asked him to go with them that night. He called him aside. His wristwatch trembled in his hand. And he whispered very gently, "Don't let him suffer, Herbal." Even so he managed to put up a show. He followed the escorts to the cell. "Painter," he said, "you can go now." The Berenguela bell had just been heard to strike midnight. "I can go at midnight?" the painter asked warily. "Come on, get out, don't make this difficult for me." The Falangists laughed, still hidden in the corridor.

Herbal found the task to be an easy one. When he killed, he simply remembered his uncle the trapper, who would even give the animals names. He called the hares Josefina and the fox Don Pedro. And besides, to tell the truth, he had respect for the man. The painter was exactly how a man should be. Going about the prison, he treated the warders as if they were ushers at a cinema.

The painter knew nothing about his guard, but Herbal knew something about him. The story went that his son, in the company of others, had thrown stones at the German's house, a German who had relations with Hitler and taught his language in Santiago. They had smashed his windowpanes. The German had gone to the police station in a rage, as if it were an international conspiracy. In no time at all the painter turned up with his son, a slight and nervous-looking boy, with eyes bigger than his hands, and reported him as one of those responsible for the stoning. Even the superintendent was amazed. He took a statement, but sent both father and son on their way.

"That's the kind of man the painter was," Herbal explained to Maria da Visitação. "He was one of the first we arrested.

'He's very dangerous,' Sergeant Landesa had said. 'Dangerous? He'd avoid stepping on an ant if he could help it.' 'What do you know?' he replied enigmatically. 'He does the posters. He's the one who paints the ideas.'"

At the time of the Rising, the most renowned Republicans were imprisoned. There were also others who were less well known, but they always coincided with the names on Sergeant Landesa's mysterious black list. The prison in Santiago, known as A Falcona, was behind Raxoi Palace, on the slope leading down from Obradoiro Square, right opposite the Cathedral, so that if you built a tunnel you would emerge in the Apostle's crypt. It was at the start of the area known as Little Hell. Every medieval cathedral, God's great temple, had a Little Hell nearby, the home of sin. Because behind the prison was Pombal, the red-light district.

The prison walls were slabs of stone coated with moss. Luckily for them, if it is possible to say such a thing, it was summer on the threshold of death. In winter, A Falcona was like an icebox and stank of mildew, the air heavy with wet leaves. But no-one there had thought as yet about winter.

For the first few days, everyone, prisoners and guards, carried on as normal, like passengers who had broken down on the slope of life, waiting for someone to crank up the engine so that they could continue their journey. Even the governor allowed relatives to visit and bring them home-made food. Meanwhile they, the detainees, seated with their backs against the walls, would while away the hours in the courtyard, chatting with apparent ease, in the jovial manner some of them had been doing only a couple of days previously, around the pedestal tables with steaming cups in the Café Español, whose walls were decorated with the painter's murals. Or like workmen on their break, ironically saluting their boss the sun with the peak of their caps, and spitting genteelly to mark their patch, heading off in search of some bread-and-water shade and after-lunch banter. Arrested in a suit or nightshirt, the long wait and the dust of the calendar were gradually making all of them in the courtyard appear the same, just as sepia does in a group portrait. We look like harvesters. We look like tramps. We look like gypsies. "No," said the painter, "we look like inmates. We are taking on the colour of prisoners."

When he was on duty, the guard Herbal could listen to what they were saying. They kept him amused like a radio. The dial of their chatter, to and fro. He would lazily sidle up to them and smoke a cigarette, leaning against the hinge of the door into the courtyard. When he had gone, they would talk about politics. "As soon as we're out of here, and we will be," Xerardo, a teacher from Porto do Son, would say, "the Republic will need refloating, as soon as there's a big enough wave. The federal Republic."

Next they would be talking about the missing link between ape and man.

"In a way," Doctor Da Barca would say with a half-smile, "human beings are the result not of improvement, but of an ailment. The mutant we descend from had to stand up on account of some pathological problem. It was clearly inferior to its quadruped ancestors. And that's without the loss of hair and tail. From the biological point of view, it was a disaster. I believe it was the chimpanzee that invented laughter the first time *Homo erectus* and it met on that stage. I mean, can you imagine? An upright, balding bloke missing his tail. Pathetic. You'd fall about laughing."

"I prefer Bible literature to literature on evolution," the painter said. "The Bible is the best script written so far of the film of the world."

"No. The best script is the one we do not know. The cell's secret poem, gentlemen!"

"Is it true what I read in the bishop's newsletter, Da Barca?" Casal intervened ironically. "That at a conference you said man hankered after his tail."

Everyone laughed, beginning with the doctor, who picked up the thread. "That's right. Apparently I also said the soul is in the thyroid gland! But now that we're about it, let me tell you something. In surgery we come across cases of dizziness and vertigo that occur when a human suddenly stands up, traces of the functional disorder brought about by the adoption of a vertical position. You see, what we humans suffer from is a kind of horizontal nostalgia. As for the tail, let's just call it a peculiarity, a biological deficiency, that man does not have one, or he does, but it's been trimmed, so to speak. The absence of a tail is a factor worth bearing in mind when discussing the origins of speech."

"What I don't understand," said the painter in amusement,

"is how you, who are so materialistic, can believe in the Holy Company of Souls."

"Hang on! I am not materialistic. It would be vulgar of me and offensive to matter, which tries so hard to come out of itself to avoid getting bored. I believe in an intelligent reality, in a supernatural environment, as it were. The erect mutant gave the chimpanzee back his laughter next to the ground. It recognized the jibe for what it was. It realized it was defective, abnormal. And that is why it also had the instinct for death. It was both plant and animal. It had and did not have roots. The great intrigue came about because of that upheaval, or peculiarity. A second nature. Another reality. What Doctor Nóvoa Santos called intelligent reality came about."

"I knew Nóvoa Santos," Casal said. "I published a book or two of his and I'd say we were good friends. He was a genius, that man. Far too good for this ungrateful country."

The mayor of Santiago, who spent his small private wealth on publishing books, paused and cast his mind back in sorrow. The poor referred to him in Galician as Novo Santo, which means New Saint. But the more rudimentary clergymen and academics hated him. One day he entered the casino in Santiago and turned the place upside down. A young boy had made a loss and committed suicide. Nóvoa's ideology was worth a constitution: be good and rebellious to a degree. The lecture he gave on being awarded the chair in Madrid was masterly and the whole auditorium, two thousand people, rose to its feet. They applauded him like an artist, like Caruso. And he had talked about the body's reflexes!

"When I was a student, I was lucky enough to attend one of his clinics," said Da Barca. "We went with him to see an old, dying man. It was a strange case. No-one could tell what was wrong with him. In Charity Hospital it was so damp your words turned mouldy in midair. As soon as he saw him, without even touching him, Don Roberto said, 'The trouble with this man is he's cold and hungry. Give him a couple of blankets and all the hot broth he can eat.'"

"But, doctor, do you really believe in the Holy Company of Souls?" Dombodán asked ingenuously.

Da Barca looked around the circle of friends, with a dramatic, investigative air.

"I believe in the Holy Company because I have seen it. It's not just a piece of local colour. One night when I was a student, I went poking about the ossuary next to Boisaca Cemetery. I had an exam and needed a sphenoid, a very complex bone in the head. An amazing bone, the sphenoid, shaped like a bat with wings! I heard something that was not a noise, as if the silence were performing a Gregorian chant. And there before my eyes was the procession of lanterns. There, if you'll forgive my pedantry, were the ectoplasmic crumbs of the dead."

The apology was unnecessary. Everyone knew what he meant. They listened carefully, though the look on their faces was increasingly one of disbelief.

"And?"

"That was it. I had my tobacco to hand, in case they asked for it. But they carried on straight past me like silent motorists."

"Where were they going?" Dombodán asked uneasily.

Doctor Da Barca adopted a serious expression, as if keen to dispel all remnants of doubt.

"Towards Eternal Indifference, my friend."

But then, seeing the effect this had on Dombodán, he added with a smile, "To tell the truth, I think they were on their way to San Andrés de Teixido, where if you don't go when alive, you must go when you have died. Yes, I think that's where they were heading."

"Let me tell you a story," the typographer Maroño broke the silence. He was a socialist and his friends called him The Good. "It's not a story. It's an incident."

"Where did it happen?"

"In Galicia," said The Good with an air of defiance. "Where else could it have been?"

"True."

"Well, there were two sisters who lived in a place called Mandouro. They lived on their own, in a bungalow left to them by their parents. From the house you could see the sea and all the ships leaving Europe bound for the South Seas. One sister was called Life and the other, Death. They were two good girls, a pleasure to look at and be with."

"The one called Death was pretty as well?" Dombodán asked with concern.

"She was. Well, she was pretty, if a bit horse-like. The point is the two of them got on very well. Since they had so many suitors, they had made a promise: they could flirt with men, even get involved, but never go their separate ways. And they kept their word. On feast days they would go down to the dance together, in the company of all the other young people in the district, to a place called Donaire. To get there, they had to cross marshland, full of mud-flats and known as Fronteira. The two sisters would wear their clogs and carry their shoes. Death's shoes were white and Life's were black."

"Don't you mean the other way round?"

"No, I mean just what I say. In reality, all the girls did what the two sisters did. They would wear their clogs and carry their shoes, so that their shoes were clean when it came to the dancing. This way, at the door of the dance, you'd get as many as a hundred pairs of clogs lined up like rowing-boats along the sand. The boys were different. The boys would ride on horseback. And perform all kinds of tricks on their mounts as they arrived and left, especially as they arrived, to impress the girls. And so time passed. The two sisters attended the dance, had the occasional fling, but always, sooner or later, they returned home.

"One night, a cold, winter's night, there was a shipwreck. As you know, there have always been and still are a lot of shipwrecks off our coast. But this was a very special shipwreck. The boat was called the *Palermo* and contained a cargo of accordions. A thousand accordions packaged in wood. The storm sank the boat and swept the cargo towards the coast. The sea, its arms like those of a crazed stevedore, smashed up the boxes and carried the accordions in towards the shore. The whole night, the accordions played tunes which you can understand were fairly sad. The music was driven in through the windows by the gale. Everyone in the district was woken and heard it, and the two sisters were scared stiff, like everyone else. In the morning, the accordions lay on the beaches like the corpses of drowned instruments. All of them were useless. All of them bar one. It was found by a young fisherman in a cave. He was so struck by the coincidence that he learned to play it. He was already a spirited, cheerful young man, but the accordion gave him an unusual grace. At the dance, Life fell for him so completely that she decided that love was worth more than the bond with her sister. And they absconded together, because Life knew that Death had a foul temper and could be very vindictive. And so she was. She has never forgiven her for it. This is why she roams to and fro, especially on stormy nights, stops at houses with clogs at the door, and asks whomever she meets, 'Do you know of a young accordionist and that slut, Life?' And because the person asked does not know, she takes them with her."

When the typographer Maroño finished the tale, the painter murmured, "Yes, I like that incident very much."

"I heard it in a bar. There are some taverns which are like universities."

"They're going to kill us all! Don't you see? They're going to kill us all!"

The person shouting was an inmate who had remained in a corner a little way off from the group, seemingly lost in his own thoughts.

"You don't stop babbling on. And what you don't realize

is that they're going to kill us. They're going to kill us all! Every single one of us!"

They looked at each other, sick at heart, not knowing what to do, as if the hot, blue August sky had shattered above them into shards of ice.

Doctor Da Barca approached him and took his wrist.

"It's all right, Baldomir, calm down. Talking is a way of letting off steam."

5

THE PAINTER HAD GOT HOLD OF A NOTEBOOK AND a carpenter's pencil. He carried it behind his ear, as they do in the trade, ready to draw at a moment's notice. The pencil had belonged to Antonio Vidal, a carpenter who called a strike in defence of the eight-hour day and used it to write a column for El Corsario. He had given it to Pepe Villaverde, a shipwright, who had a daughter called Mariquiña and another named Fraternidade. Villaverde was a self-confessed libertarian and humanist, and would open his speeches on the factory floor talking of love, "We live in communism if, and in proportion to how much, we love each other." When he became a timekeeper on the railways, Villaverde gave the pencil to his friend in the trade union, also a carpenter, Marcial Villamor. And before he was killed by the escorts who would swoop down on A Falcona, Marcial gave the pencil to the painter when he saw him trying to draw the Pórtico da Gloria with a piece of slate.

As the days went by, trailing the worst omens in their

wake, the painter concentrated more and more on the notebook. While the others chatted, he tirelessly copied down their features. He sought their profile, a particular gesture or look, the areas of shade. And he did so with more and more dedication, almost feverishly, as if in response to an urgent request.

The painter would then explain who was who on the old façade.

The Cathedral was a few feet away, but the guard Herbal had only visited it twice. Once, as a child, when his parents had come from the village to sell cabbage and onion seed on Saint James's Day. From that time he remembered they had taken him to the Saint of the Bumps and he had placed his fingers in the carved-out shape of a hand and been told to bang his forehead against the stone crown. He had been captivated, however, by the blind man's eyes of the saint and it was his father who, with that toothless grin, grabbed him by the scruff of the neck and made him see stars. "If he doesn't do it himself," his mother said, "he won't get the inspiration." "Don't you worry," said his father, "he won't get it anyway." The second time he went was in a uniform, to an offertory Mass. The nave was bristling with people, they had Latin coming out of every pore. But what amazed him was the Botafumeiro. This he remembered well. The huge censer shrouded the altar in mist, as if the whole thing were a strange story.

The painter would talk about the Pórtico da Gloria. He had drawn it with the thick, red pencil he always carried, like a carpenter, behind his ear. Each of the figures in the drawing turned out to be one of his friends from A Falcona. "You, Casal," he said to the former mayor of Santiago, "you're Moses with the Tables of the Law. You, Pasín," he said to one who was in the union of railwaymen, "you're Saint John the Evangelist, with his feet on top of the eagle. Saint Paul, that's you, my captain," he said to Lieutenant Martínez, who had been a border guard and then a councillor under the Republic. Then there were two old inmates, Ferreiro of Zas and González of Cesures, and he told them they were the elders at the top, in the centre, with the organistrum in the orchestra of the Apocalypse. And he told Dombodán, who was the youngest and a bit naive, that he was an angel playing the trumpet. He went around everyone and showed them their likeness on the sheet. And he explained that the base of the Pórtico da Gloria was full of monsters, with talons and beaks like birds of prey, and hearing this they all went quiet, a silence that gave them away, because Herbal could feel their gaze fixed on his silhouette as he stood there, a silent witness. And finally the painter spoke about the prophet Daniel, who it would seem was the only one smiling unashamedly on the old façade. An artistic marvel, a mystery to the experts. "That, Da Barca, is you."

6

ONE DAY THE PAINTER HAD GONE TO PAINT THE lunatics in the asylum at Conxo. He wanted to capture the landscapes ploughed on their faces by psychic pain, not from morbidity, but out of an awful fascination. Mental illness, the painter thought, provokes in us an expulsive reaction. Fear before the madman precedes compassion, which sometimes never arrives. It seemed to him this might be because we sense that illness as part of a kind of common soul, out there on the loose waiting to pick off bodies as they come along. Hence the tendency to hide the sufferer away. The painter could remember a room in a house next door that was always closed. One day he heard wailing and asked who was in there. The lady of the house replied, "No-one."

The painter wanted to capture the invisible wounds of existence.

The scene in the asylum was horrifying. Not because the inmates approached him in a threatening way. Very few of them had done that, and in a way that was more like a ritual, as if they were trying to shake off an allegory. What amazed the painter was the expression of those who were not looking. Their renunciation of space, the absolute nothingness they were walking through.

His mind in his hand, he had stopped feeling afraid. With his brush strokes he followed the line of anguish, stupefaction, delirium. His hand spiralled feverishly between the walls. The painter came to momentarily and looked at his watch. It was a while since he had been due to leave and already getting dark. He picked up his notebook and made his way towards the lodge. The door had been bolted with a huge padlock and there was no-one to be seen. The painter called out for the porter, gently at first and then out loud. He heard the clock strike in the church. Nine o'clock in the evening. He was half an hour late, it was not that long. What if they had forgotten all about him? A madman stood in the garden with his arms around the trunk of a box-tree. The painter thought it must be two hundred years old, that tree, and the man needed somewhere to hold on to.

The minutes passed and the painter saw himself shouting in anguish and the inmate moored to the box-tree viewed him with fraternal pity.

At this point a smiling man appeared, young but wearing a suit, and asked him what was wrong. The painter told him he was a painter, that he had been allowed in to portray the patients, and he had not realized what time it was. The young man in a suit adopted a very serious expression, "That's exactly what happened to me."

And he added,

"And I've been shut up in here for two years now."

The painter could see his own eyes. Snow-white, with a solitary wolf on the horizon.

"But I'm not mad!"

"That's exactly what I said."

Seeing he was on the verge of panicking, he smiled and revealed who he was, "It's only a joke. I'm a doctor. Don't worry, we'll be out of here in a trice."

And so the painter met Doctor Da Barca. It was the beginning of a great friendship.

The guard looked at him from the semi-darkness, as he had done so many times before.

"I also knew the doctor very well," Herbal told Maria da Visitação. "Very well. He never could have suspected how much I knew about him. For a long period I was his shadow. I tracked him like a gun dog. He was my man."

It was after the elections in February 1936, which were won by the Frente Popular. Sergeant Landesa assembled in secret a group of men he could rely on and the first thing he told them was that this meeting had never taken place. "Get this into your heads. What is spoken here was never spoken. There are no orders, no instructions, no bosses. Nothing. I am the only one that exists and I am the Holy Spirit. I don't want any crap. From now on, you are shadows and shadows do not crap or crap white like seagulls. I want you to write me a novel on every one of these elements. I want to know it all." When he spread out the list with the objectives they were to stick close to, names of public and other, unknown figures, the guard Herbal became aware of a burning sensation on his tongue. One of those on the list was Doctor Da Barca. "I can take care of this one, sergeant. I'm already on to him." "But does he know you?" "No, he doesn't even know that I exist." "Just remember that there's nothing personal, information is all that is required."

"There's nothing personal, sergeant," Herbal lied. "I shall be invisible. I'm not much good at writing, but you'll have a novel on the man."

"I am led to believe he's quite a preacher."

"He's a bomb waiting to go off, sergeant."

"Good. In which case go ahead."

From that meeting that never existed, some time later Herbal would remember – once more the sound of memory like the murmur of the fountain where the guts are washed – the moment when someone referred to the painter. "He's not a house painter," Sergeant Landesa informed the agent finally put in charge of his surveillance. "This one paints ideas. Lives round at the Madame's." Everyone had laughed. Everyone but Herbal, who did not know the reason and did not ask. Years later he would find out from the deceased. A madame was the old whore who taught the young girls their trade. She taught them above all how to carry the weight of the man on their bodies for as little time as possible and the golden rule, which was to charge before offering their services. "From time to time," the dead man told him, "people would still knock at the door. Fathers and mothers with a young girl asking for the madame. My wife would bite her tongue, tell them there was no madame living there any more. And then she would cry. She would cry for each and every one of them. And she was right. Very near there, in Pombal Street, they would find the madame they were looking for."

Four months after the meeting, at the end of June, Herbal handed in his report on Doctor Da Barca. The sergeant weighed it in his hand. "Why, it does seem like a novel." There was a folder with a pile of notes, written by hand in a tortuous script. The ink smudges everywhere, which blotting paper had sealed and turned into scars, looked like traces of a tiresome fight. Had they not been blue, you would have thought they were drops of blood fallen from the scribe's brow. In a single paragraph, the letters above the line leaned over in different directions, to the left and to the right, like ideograms of a fleet bowed by the wind.

Sergeant Landesa started reading from a page at random. "What does this say? Lesson in *autonomy* with a corpse!" he exclaimed scornfully. "Anatomy, Herbal, anatomy."

"I've already told you I wasn't very good at writing," the guard cut in, somewhat offended.

"Another note, 'Lesson in death throes. Clapping.' And what's this?"

"That was a professor, sir, Da Barca's boss. He lay down on a table and showed how the dead breathed before dying, in dual time. He talked about this thing some people get when they're dying, a sort of hallucination that helps them to pass away in peace. He said that the body was very wise.

And pretended to be dead as in the theatre. The applause went on for quite a while."

"Well, I'll have to go and see him," remarked the sergeant sarcastically. And then he asked in some surprise, "And what does it say here?" He read with difficulty, "Corrump . . . corruptive beauty?"

"Let me see," said Herbal, moving closer to read over his shoulder. His voice trembled as he recognized the words he himself had written. "Consumptive beauty, sir.

"He – I mean the doctor – examined a sick young girl from Local Welfare in front of the students. First of all he asked her questions. What her name was, where she was from. Lucinda, from Valdemar. And he would tell her what a lovely name, what a lovely spot. Then he took her by the wrist and looked into her eyes. He told the students that the eyes were the windows of the mind. Then he did that thing they do, tapping here and there with his fingers."

Herbal fell silent for a moment and stared into space. He was again recreating that scene that had both disturbed and astonished him. The girl in the thin nightdress. The sensation that he had seen her before, combing her hair in a window. The doctor delicately placing two fingers of his left hand and percussing with his right middle finger. "The elbow should not move. Appreciate the purity of sound. Like this." Tock. Tock. Hmm. Not a tock or a drum. And then with that instrument, the one for the ears, on the same parts of the body. On the lungs. Hmm. "Thank you, Lucinda, you can get dressed now. It's a bit cold. Everything will be fine, you'll see." When she has gone, he tells the students, "It is the sound of a chipped pot. Though really none of this would be necessary. Her pale, drawn face. A slight colour in her cheeks. The varnish of sweat in this cold hall. The melancholy gaze. That consumptive beauty."

"Tuberculosis, doctor!" shouted a student in the first row.

"Exactly." And he added in a bitter tone, "Koch's bacillus sowing tubercles in the rosy garden."

Herbal felt the stethoscope's cold tentacle on his chest. A voice shouted, "It has the sound of a chipped pot!"

"Consumptive beauty. The phrase attracted my attention, sergeant. So I copied it down."

"Wasn't it a bit rash to go to the faculty?"

"I went in with a group of Portuguese students on a visit. I wanted to find out if he indoctrinated in class."

The sergeant did not look up again from the papers until he had finished reading. He seemed enchanted by the story unfolding and would murmur from time to time as he went along. "So he's Cuban, is he?" "That's right, sir, the son of returned emigrants." "He likes to dress up?" "Cuts a dashing figure. Though he can't have more than one suit, sergeant, and a couple of bow ties. He never wears an overcoat or a hat." "He's only twenty-four?" "He looks older, sir. He sometimes grows a beard." "It says here the maimed raise their stumps like fists. The man must speak well." "He's better than a priest, sir." "What about this young Miss Marisa Mallo? She sounds interesting." Herbal was silent.

"Is she something to look at?"

33

"She's very pretty, yes, but she's not involved."

"In what?"

"In his business, sir."

The sergeant flicked through some newspaper cuttings which Herbal had included in his report: "The soul's substratum and intelligent reality." "Children's coffins in the time of Charles Dickens." "Millet's painting, washerwomen's hands and a woman's invisibility." "Hell in Dante, the painting *Mad Kate* and the asylum at Conxo." "The problem of State, basic confidence and Rosalía de Castro's poem 'Justice by the Hand'[1]." "The landscape's *engram* and the feeling of homesickness." "The horror to come: genetic biology, the fanatical desire to be healthy and the concept of *ballast lives*." The sergeant viewed with circumspection the same signature under each article: Dr Barkowsky.

"So it's Barkowsky, is it? It would seem," he said, "your man never stops. Doctor for Local Welfare. Assistant in the Faculty of Medicine. Delivers pamphlets, conferences and meetings. Goes from the Hospital to the Republican Centre and still has time to take his girlfriend to the cinema in the Teatro Principal. He's a close friend of the pro-Galician painter who does the posters. He meets with Republicans, Anarchists, Socialists, Communists . . . what the hell is this guy?"

"I think he's a bit of everything, my sergeant."

"Anarchists and Communists are constantly at each other's throats. The other day, at the tobacco factory in Coruña, they

1 See Appendix I.

34

almost came to blows. A strange creature, this Da Barca fellow!"

"He seems to act on his own. As a link."

"Well, don't take your eye off him. He's clearly up to no good!"

There, in clumsy, handcrafted terms that made it more useful and reliable, was everything there would be to know about a man. The friendships he had, the routes he took, the brand of tobacco he smoked.

The guard Herbal knew the doctor very well, though he never could have imagined it. He had tracked him for some time, not under orders but through need. You could say he had followed him like a sick dog, sniffing out his footsteps. He hated Doctor Da Barca. It was not long since he had graduated and already he had a reputation for being a great medical talent. That and a revolutionary. At meetings in different towns he spoke Galician with a Cuban accent, having been born there of an emigrant family, and he had that special way of preaching, like a bomb waiting to go off, that made cripples stand up and even the maimed raise their fists. He would say that the battle to be waged was against melancholy.

A lot of people did not understand the doctrines of politicians, but melancholy was something people did understand. Herbal had been taken ill as a child. He had turned green, an ugly green colour like fiddle-dock, and swelled, so that he waddled like a duck. He was led from one healer to another, until one of them told his father to immerse him in water sprinkled with tobacco. And this is what he did. He was convinced, on account of previous occurrences that are not worth going into here, that his father was capable of drowning him. He spun around and bit him on the hand. And then his father got even more annoyed. "You son of a whore!" he cursed, and dropped him full into the cask with the brew. He kept him there under the water right up until he saw that his arms had stopped flailing.

"As soon as I came out, I went this tobacco colour and shot up, all skin, like a razor-shell, the way I am today."

Yes, he understood very well what was discussed at those meetings of the Frente Popular. The first time he had really left the village was to do military service. That for him had been like a breath of fresh air. Aside from the odd short leave, the only time he had gone back was to bury his parents. As a serving soldier he had formed part of the troops led by General Franco when he stifled – this was the word every-one used – the miners' revolt in Asturias of 1934. A woman, kneeling before the body of her husband, had shouted with tears in her eyes, "Soldier, you're one of the people as well!" "Yes," he thought, "that's true." Damn people, damn misery. From now on he would try to earn a wage for his services. He became a guard.

Doctor Da Barca was right. His melancholy would not be long coming. Herbal was one of those who arrested him, who in fact overpowered him, bringing down the butt of his rifle on the back of his neck. Daniel Da Barca was tall, he had a fire burning in his chest. Everything about him was assertive: his forehead, his Jewish nose, his mouth, its fleshy lips. When he expressed himself, he would spread his arms like wings and his fingers seemed to speak for the dumb.

During the first days of the Rising, he had stayed away. It was only a matter of waiting until he grew confident and thought that the hunt had eased up. When he did finally return to his mother's house, the five of them in the patrol jumped on top of him and he resisted like a wild boar. His mother shouted like a madwoman from the window. But what riled the soldiers most of all was when the seamstresses came out of a shop opposite. They cursed them, they spat on them, and one or two of those little seamstresses actually dared to pull at their trench coats and scratch their necks. Doctor Da Barca was bleeding from the nose, the mouth, the ears, but he would not give up. Until he, the guard Herbal, caught him on the head and knocked him to the ground.

"And then I turned round to face the seamstresses and aimed at their stomachs. And had it not been for Sergeant Landesa, I don't know what I would have done, because if there was one thing that got me it was those girls shouting for him like a chorus of mourners. The bit about the mother I could understand, but with them I saw red. And that is when I let go of what was gnawing at me, 'What the fuck is it about this guy? What do you care? Sluts, you're a bunch of sluts!' Sergeant Landesa took hold of me and said, 'Come on, Herbal, we've still got work to do.'"

7

DOCTOR DA BARCA HAD A GIRLFRIEND. AND THAT girlfriend was the most beautiful woman in the world. In the world that Herbal had seen and, he was sure, in the one he had not seen. Marisa Mallo. He was the son of poor peasant farmers. In his house in the village there were very few pretty things. He remembered it without nostalgia, full of smoke or flies. Like a pipeline stretched across time, the memory stank of manure and carbide gas. Beginning with the walls, everything had a patina like rancid bacon, a sooty yellow colour that got in the eyes. In the morning, when he left with the cows, he saw everything through those sooty yellow glasses. He even saw the green meadows in this way. But there were two things in the house he looked upon as treasures. One was his little sister, Beatriz, a blonde, blue-eyed girl, who always had a cold and a runny nose. The other was an old quince tin where mother kept her jewellery: some jet earrings, a rosary, a medal made of Venezuelan gold as soft as chocolate, a silver peso from the reign of Alfonso XII, which she had inherited from her father, and some mother-of-pearl hairslides. There was also a little jar with two aspirin and his first tooth.

He would place the tooth in the palm of his hand and to him it resembled a grain of rye which a mouse had nibbled. But the really pretty object was the old tinplate box, which had gone rusty at the joins. On the lid was the image of a young woman with a fruit in her hand, a back comb in her hair, and a red dress with a pattern of white flowers and flounces on the sleeves. The first time he saw Marisa Mallo, it was as if she had descended from the quince box to stroll about the main market-place in Fronteira. They had gone there to sell a pig and some early potatoes. It was two miles from the village to the town on foot along muddy tracks. His father went in front, with his felt hat and daughter in his arms, his mother went behind, carrying the heavy basket on her head, and he was in the middle, pulling at the pig, which was tied with a halter around its leg. To his despair, the animal kept trying to nuzzle into the mud and when they reached Fronteira it looked like a large mole. His father slapped him across the face. "Who's going to buy this pig now?" And there he was, at the market, wiping away the encrusted dirt with a handful of straw when he lifted his head and saw her go by. She stood out like a young woman from the cluster of other girls, who seemed to accompany her only in order to point to her and say here is the queen. They came and went like a band of butterflies and he followed them with his eyes, while his father blasphemed because no-one was going to buy that scruffy pig, and it was all his fault. He dreamt that the pig was a lamb and she came and ran her fingers through its curls. "We should be selling you, not the pig," his father would mutter. "Though I doubt anyone would want you."

"That's just the way my father was. If he started the day cursing, there was no going back, like someone constantly digging a cesspit under their feet. And I would think to myself yes, please, if someone could come and buy me and take me away with a string tied to my leg."

In the end, they sold the pig and the new potatoes. And mother was able to buy a tin of oil with the image of another woman, who also looked like Marisa Mallo. They returned to the main market in Fronteira on many other occasions. He no longer cared about his father's mood. To him these days were like holidays, the only ones with any sense in the whole year. Putting out the cows to graze, he would yearn for the first day of the month to arrive. And this is how he observed the growing and blooming of Marisa Mallo, member of the region's powerful families, goddaughter to the mayor, daughter to the notary, little sister to the parish priest in Fronteira. And, above all, Don Benito Mallo's grandchild. And he never had a lamb to see if she would come and comb its woollen curls.

8

IT WAS IN THE CAR, ON THE WAY BACK FROM THE
outing with the painter, while the rest of the party passed
around a bottle of brandy, that he noticed for the first time
the disorder in his head. As if there were people inside it.
The Falangists had gone from being very annoyed to being
hysterical and were patting him on the shoulder. "Drink
up, boy, drink." But he told them he did not drink. And they
burst out laughing. "Since when, Herbal?" And he replied
very seriously that he had never drunk. "I don't like alcohol."
"But you're always half-cut!" "Leave him alone," said the
driver, "he's a bit strange tonight. Even his voice seems to
have changed."

And that was the last he spoke. He had heard a shot
and sunk to the ground. Along the funnel of a very straight
road he worked on his drawing of the Pórtico da Gloria with
a carpenter's pencil. And he did it with incredible skill.
He was able to describe it with words he had never used.
"The beauty of the angels bearing the instruments of the

41

Passion," his head was telling him, "is an aching beauty that demonstrates the melancholy at the unjust death of the Son of God." When he drew the prophet Daniel, he managed to capture the happy smile of the stone and, as he followed his gaze, he became aware of the enigma. Carrying the food, across Obradoiro Square, cloaked in the sun's rays, with a white cloth over her basket, was Marisa Mallo.

"How did it go yesterday, Herbal?" the governor asked gloomily.

"He was a Nazarene, sir."

He became aware that the governor was looking at him in a strange way and recalled what the others had said the night before, about his voice having changed. In future, it was better to keep quiet. Stick to monosyllables. Yes, no, sir.

When Marisa Mallo came in with the food and said good morning, he replied with a grunt and an abrupt gesture that meant you can leave the basket there, I shall be making my inspection. As soon as he lifted the cloth, he saw the local cheese, wrapped in a cabbage leaf. "That's where the butt is," the sight in his head told him. The following day she returned with the basket and he saw the drum of the revolver in a sponge cake, and he gestured that everything was OK, that the basket should come through. The third day he already knew that the barrel was in the bread. And he waited with curiosity for the next delivery, the morning Marisa arrived with bags under her eyes he had not noticed before, because he finally looked straight at her, and dared to undress her from top to toe, as if she were cheese, sponge cake and bread. "I've got some trout," she said. And he saw a bullet in each trout's belly and said, "OK, I'll pass them on to him, you can go now."

Until then he had avoided Marisa Mallo's eyes. His head bowed, he fixed his gaze on her wrists. And it hurt him to know that what was being rumoured was true. That she had cut her wrists when her relations, the leading family in Fronteira, tried by every possible means to erase Doctor Da Barca from her mind. Marisa Mallo was all skin and bones. Marisa Mallo wore hospital bandages in place of bracelets. Marisa Mallo was prepared to die for Doctor Da Barca. It was then he went to the guardroom and very discreetly swapped the bullets for some of a different calibre. Under the darkness of night, when he assembled the revolver and tried to fill the drum, Doctor Da Barca knew that the attempt to escape had failed. Under the flagstone that, to the astonishment of the other inmates, he had managed to turn over, he hid for ever a revolver with bullets that could not be used.

The escorts came for him a few nights later. There were people from Fronteira who knew him well and were out to get him. Among the party there was also a medical student who had failed. But Herbal did not allow them into the cells. The voice in his head prompted him. "Tell them he's not here any more, funnily enough he was taken to Coruña this afternoon." "Funny that. The one you're after," he said, "was put on trial and driven straight to Coruña today. I can't say I envy him." Since the others had a particular prisoner in their sights and were clearly under orders, he pretended to slit his throat. "Some names have been carefully chosen to serve as an example. They'll be dealt with in a day or two in Campo da Rata. Don't you worry. And long live Spain."

This was not entirely untrue, there had been several urgent transfers to the prison in Coruña over the last couple of days. That night, Herbal went to the governor's office and sifted through the files until he found the transfer papers. Three schoolteachers were due to be moved the following day. The dead man told him, "Take the warrant, now the governor's pen, and write Da Barca's full name in the blank space. Don't worry, I'll help you with the handwriting."

The following day, when Doctor Da Barca passed him in the doorway, bound for his new destination, in handcuffs and with no other belongings than the bag he had used as a doctor, he noticed how he fixed him with a stern gaze, eyes that said, "I shan't forget you, razor-shell, who murdered the painter. May you live long enough for the virus of remorse and rot to spread till you gently explode." When Marisa Mallo came, at visiting time, he told her he was not there any more, the one you're asking for is not on the list, and gave no further explanations, as cold as can be, as if the person in question were a total stranger who had disappeared in time. And all because he wanted to see how sad the most beautiful woman could be. To see how tears spring from an inaccessible source. After a few seconds lasting an eternity, like someone catching a very fine piece of porcelain in the air just before it smashes, he added, "He's in Coruña. Alive."

That same day, he went to see Sergeant Landesa. "My sergeant, I should like to ask a very personal favour." "What is it, Herbal?" Sergeant Landesa held him in esteem. He had always carried out orders without a second thought. They understood each other well. They had trodden gorse together as kids. "Well, my sergeant, you see, I wondered if you might arrange for my transfer to Coruña. My sister lives there, she has a husband who beats her, and would take me in to keep him under control." "That's as good as done, Herbal. Give him a kick in the balls from me." He signed and stamped a piece of paper, because for some reason Sergeant Landesa held more power than his rank would imply. From there he went straight to see the officer in charge of approving transfers within the corps. This was a suspicious man, of the kind who believes that their task of putting obstacles in the way is a momentous one. When he explained that he was interested in a move to the prison in Coruña, the officer interrupted him, rose from his office chair and delivered a heated discourse. "We are fighting a relentless war against evil, the salvation of Christendom depends on our victory, thousands of men are risking their lives at this very moment in the trenches. And meanwhile what are we up to? Processing applications. Mincing bullshit. Volunteers, volunteers to fight for God and country, that's what I should like to have right here, in a line, at the door to this office." It was then he gave him the piece of paper Sergeant Landesa had signed. The blood drained from the officer's cheeks. "Why on earth didn't you tell me before it was from the information service?" The painter, as if amused by the whole incident, whispered in his ear, "Tell him it is not your task to deliver discourses." But he remained silent. "Report first thing tomorrow at your new destination. And forget what I said. The main struggle is waged in the rearguard."

9

AT THE PRISON IN CORUÑA THERE WERE HUNDREDS
of inmates. Everything seemed to work in an organized,
more industrial way. Even the outings at night. They were
taken on foot to Campo da Rata, by the sea-shore. Sometimes,
during the volleys of firing, the prisoners who wore white
shirts would shine out in the sails of light emanating from
Hercules Lighthouse. The sea would low along the cliffs
from Punta Herminia to San Amaro, like a deranged cow at
the windows of the empty feeding troughs. After each volley,
a silence of human lament would be heard. Until the litany
of the mad cow started up again.

One of the ways in which the night escorts entertained
themselves was by postponing death. Sometimes, from
among the prisoners who had been selected to be murdered,
one remained alive. That piece of luck, that random life,
made everything even more dramatic, before and afterwards.
Before, because a tiny and capricious ray of hope impeded
the sympathy of those in the line, like pebbles along the

route. Afterwards, because the one who came back would certify the horror in the terror of his eyes.

One evening at the beginning of September, he was standing on his own in a watchtower, following a cormorant in flight, when the painter's voice spoke to him, "Try and be a volunteer tonight." Unafraid that he might be heard, he replied angrily, "Go to hell." "But, Herbal, surely you're not going to leave him now?" "Go to hell, painter, haven't you seen the way he looks at me? It's like he's sticking two syringes in my eyes. When Marisa comes to see him, he reckons it's out of choice I stand in the middle listening to what they say and not even letting them touch fingertips. His trouble is that he's no idea what an order is!" "Well," the painter told him, "you could turn the occasional blind eye." "I have done, you know I have, I let them touch each other's fingertips."

"And what would they say to each other?" Maria da Visitação asked, joining her fingertips.

"There was a lot of noise. There were so many inmates and visitors they couldn't make themselves heard even at the top of their voices. They would come out with the sort of things lovers say, but a bit stranger.

"He said that, as soon as he was free, he would go to Oporto, to Bolhão Market, and buy her a bag of coloured beans called marvels.

"She said she would buy him a bag of hours. She knew of a trader in Valença who sold hours of lost time.

"He said they would have a baby girl and she would turn out to be a poet.

"She said she had dreamt they had already had a baby boy years ago, he had taken off on a boat and was now a violinist in America.

"And I thought these were hardly worthwhile occupations at such a time."

That night, Herbal was waiting to go as a volunteer with the escorts when it was time for the outing. This was a curious fact. It was never announced but, as if it had something to do with the moon, everyone knew when it was a night of blood. In the firing squad, with Doctor Da Barca in front of him, he pretended to care even less, as if he were setting eyes on him for the first time. But then, when he aimed, he remembered his uncle the trapper and said with his look, "I wish I didn't have to, my friend." The prisoners, well versed in the art of martyrdom, tried to remain upright on the piles of rubbish in Campo da Rata, but the strong sea breeze made them flap like clothes hung from the cable of a ship. The first to shoot, to open the season, waited for a sail of light to pass, so that there would be a longer period of darkness. It felt as if they were firing into the wind. A little stronger and a gust of the north-easterly would bring down the dead on top of them.

Doctor Da Barca continued to remain upright.

"Take him," the painter whispered urgently in his ear. "Move!"

"This one's coming back!" Herbal said. And he snatched at him swiftly like a hunter carrying a live wood pigeon by the wings.

Anyone who returned from the journey to death became part of a different order of existence. They would sometimes lose their mind and power of speech on the way. To the escorts themselves, they became a kind of invisible, immune being, who had to be ignored for some time until they resumed their mortal nature.

But Doctor Da Barca was sought again after only a couple of days.

"Wake up, didn't you hear the bolts?" the painter alerted Herbal, shaking him by the ear. "Uh-uh, not this time," the guard said to the voice. "That's it. Leave me alone. If he has to die, I hope he's struck down on the spot." "Listen. Are you going to give up now? You've no risk involved," said the painter. "I haven't?" Herbal replied, on the verge of shouting. "I'm almost going mad, or doesn't that seem much to you?" "It's not bad for a time like this," said the painter laconically.

The guards at the main gate had let a group of escorts into the prison, people he did not know, except for one who sent a shiver running down his spine, he who had seen it all before: a priest he had come across at an official ceremony, now wearing a blue shirt and with a pistol on his belt. They scoured corridors and cells, picking off men from a list. "Is that everyone?" "There's one missing. Daniel Da Barca." The muffled silence of a wake. The torch lit up a bulge on the ground. Dombodán. Herbal saying, "That must be him." But then, the ghost's determined voice, "Who is it you're after?" "Daniel Da Barca." "Yes, that's me, over here."

"Now what?" Herbal asks, unsure what to do. "Follow

them, you fool!" the painter tells him.

The word went around the cells. Doctor Da Barca was being taken out for a second time. As if this were as far as misfortune could go, the prison spewed out all the pent-up shouts of despair and rage from that never-ending summer of 1936. The pipes, the bars, the walls, a fierce percussion affecting men and things.

On the way, on the shore of San Amaro Beach, Herbal was saying, "This one's mine. A personal matter."

He dragged Doctor Da Barca down to the sand, punched him in the stomach and brought him to his knees. He grabbed his hair, "Open your mouth, for Christ's sake." The barrel between his teeth. "Better not break them," thought the doctor. He put the barrel in his mouth. At the last moment he lowered the trajectory.

"One queer less," he said.

In the morning some washerwomen found him. They cleaned his wounds with sea water. They were disturbed by some soldiers. "Where did this one come from?" "Where do you think? From the prison, like all the rest." They gestured towards the dead. "What are you going to do with him?" the women asked. "Take him back, what else are we going to do? Get our balls chopped off?"

"Poor man! Is there no God in heaven?"

Doctor Da Barca had a clean wound. The bullet had come out the back of his neck without affecting any vital organ. "He's lost a lot of blood," said Doctor Soláns, "but with a bit of luck he'll heal."

"Mother of God! It makes me want to believe in a miracle, a message. Even in hell there are certain rules," the prison chaplain remarked. "Wait until the court-martial. Then they can shoot him as God intended."

The conversation was being held in the governor's office. The governor was equally ill at ease, "I don't know what's going on at the top, but they're very anxious. They think this Doctor Da Barca should have been dead some time ago, when the Movement started. They don't want him being brought to trial. It would seem he has dual nationality and the whole thing could get quite out of hand."

He approached the office window. In the distance, near Hercules Tower, a stonemason was chiselling stone crosses. "In confidence, Father, I shall tell you what I know. They don't care how it's done, they want him out of the picture. Incidentally, he has a girlfriend, quite lovely to look at. A real beauty, believe me. Still. The dead who don't die are difficult to deal with."

"The man's alive," said Doctor Soláns with strange resolve. "I took an oath and I plan to keep it. His health now depends on me."

During the days it took for him to recover, Doctor Soláns remained on duty in the infirmary. At night, he would lock the door from the inside. When Doctor Da Barca was able to speak, they discovered some common ground: Doctor Nóvoa Santos's *General Pathology*.

"By the way, Father," the governor said, now that they were on more familiar terms, "what do the two of you think about Dombodán, the one they call The Kid?"

"Think, why?" said the priest.

"He's been sentenced to death. But we all know he's just a bit retarded. The village idiot."

10

IN PRISON, THE BEST SIGN OF FRIENDSHIP WAS HELPING someone to delouse. As a mother would help her child.

Soap was impossible to get hold of and clothes were washed using only water, in very short supply. It took a patient hand to remove the parasites and nits. The second most abundant fauna in jail were rats. Tame rats. At night, they scoured the bulges of dreams on the ground. What on earth did they eat? "Dreams," Doctor Da Barca would say. "They nibble at our dreams. Rats feed equally off the underworld and the overworld."

The prison also had a cricket, which Dombodán had found in the courtyard. He had made a small house for it out of cardboard, with the door always open. It would sing day and night on the table in the infirmary.

When he got better, Doctor Da Barca was court-martialled and sentenced to death. He was considered to be one of the leaders of the Frente Popular, a political coalition that was "anti-Spain", part of the propaganda apparatus that favoured the Statute of Autonomy for Galicia, of "separatist" tendency, and one of the brains behind the "revolutionary committee" that organized the resistance to the "glorious Movement" of 1936.

For months, those who had recently come to power were deadlocked. News of Doctor Da Barca's case had spread abroad and an international campaign was under way for him to be granted a reprieve. The insurgents were by no means sensitive to such appeals, but in this case there was a factor that made it difficult to carry out the sentence. Since the defendant had been born in Cuba, he had dual nationality. The Cuban government was an ally of Franco, but the press there were asking for clemency in conspicuous headlines. Even the more conservative sectors were moved by the story of that man who had escaped the clutches of death with miraculous stubbornness. In the long wait, as if secret radio waves were crossing the Atlantic, the news reports peeled off details from the trial, underlining the elegance of the young physician as against a tribunal of men in arms. The version most frequently given claimed he had ended his speech with verses that had shaken the courtroom.

> This is Spain! She is stunned and badly treated
> under the brutal weight of her misfortune.

In a well-intentioned but probably apocryphal brush stroke, given the colourful propensity for which the author of the report was famous, the doctor was even credited with a fitting invocation to José Martí to complement his plea.

No thistle or nettle grows
for the cruel man who would wrest
the heart from inside my chest:
For him I grow a white rose.

"It was said later on he'd recited some verses and been interrupted sabre in hand, but I was there and it wasn't like that," Herbal told Maria da Visitação. "Doctor Da Barca didn't recite any verses. Standing up, he spoke the whole time in a slow, deliberate tone of voice, as if restraining an eager child, which made the tribunal feel awkward right from the start. He'd only been given permission to speak as a formality. The members of the tribunal had one foot out of the hall. He began with some comments about justice which I'd say he was making up, but you could get the gist. And then he spoke about lemons and Dombodán. Dombodán was a big lad, good as bread and just a little bit retarded, one of those we call the innocents hereabouts. He was arrested with some miners from Lousame on their way to defend Coruña with dynamite. He'd joined them on the lorry and they'd let him, because Dombodán would always follow the miners wherever they went, like a mascot. He was waiting in chapel to be executed. He didn't even understand that he was about to be killed. Doctor Da Barca didn't say a word about himself, and I think that's what annoyed the tribunal the most. That and the fact it was lunchtime."

"Gentlemen of the tribunal," Doctor Da Barca had said, "justice belongs to the field of the soul's forces. Hence it can appear in the most unlikely places. If you call for it, it will come. It may have a bandage over its eyes, but it will be able to listen. We cannot know for certain where it has come from, like something preceding judges, the accused and the written laws themselves." "Get to the point," the presiding judge said with a note of severity, "this is not an Athenaeum." "Of course, sir. At the time of the great sea voyages, the primary cause of mortality was scurvy, more than shipwrecks and naval warfare. Hence it became known as 'this foul and fatal mischief'. On long journeys, only twenty out of every hundred made it back alive. Halfway through the 18th century, Captain James Cook included a cask of lemon juice among his supplies and discovered that … " "I'm going to withdraw the permission to speak." "But, sir, this is my testament." "I don't think you're so old that we have to go back to Christopher Columbus." "All that is needed, gentlemen, to circumvent hardship that has not been pronounced by any tribunal is a small provision of lemons. I have tried through various channels to obtain them, as well as bandages and iodine, given that the infirmary … " "Have you quite finished?" "Sir, as far as I am concerned, modesty aside, I should like to offer an extenuating circumstance. I have used this unexpected break from my captivity for a spot of analysis and have discovered, not without surprise on my part, a psychic anomaly. When it comes to health, even we doctors are unable to pull the wool over our eyes. My case might best be described as a slight but chronic mental handicap, the result possibly of a difficult birth or a poor diet in my childhood. Some people in the same situation, but without the same emotional support, were mistakenly thought of as lunatics and admitted to the asylum at Conxo. I was taken in by the community, who made some room for me, gave me jobs to do that were infinitely childlike, such as going to the fountain for water or to the oven for bread, jobs that might require the driving force hidden beneath my docility, such as carrying wood for the fireplace, stones for a wall and even a calf in my arms. In payment, with subtle wisdom, the people called me an innocent instead of an idiot. The miners considered me their friend. They bought me drinks in the bar, took me to festivities, and I would drink and dance as if I left work alongside them every day. Wherever they went, I would follow. And they never called me an idiot. That, gentlemen of the tribunal, is I, an innocent. Dombodán, The Kid."

Dombodán's name echoed like a firework in the belly of the courtroom. The presiding judge rose to his feet, visibly shaken, and ordered Doctor Da Barca to be quiet, laying hand to his sabre. "Enough theatre. The trial is over. Ready for sentencing." They would willingly have buried him there and then.

11

THE INTERNATIONAL CAMPAIGN FOR ONCE BORE
fruit. At the last moment. In response to the government
of Cuba's request, Doctor Da Barca had his death sentence
commuted to one of life imprisonment.

"In that way he had, he had made himself the prison
first-aider, so to speak," Herbal told Maria da Visitação. "He
was like one of those healers who cure warts from a distance
simply by reciting a couple of verses. Even when he had one
foot in the grave and was waiting to be executed, he carried
on boosting everyone else's spirits."

The political prisoners functioned as a kind of commune.
People who would not talk to each other in the street, who
really hated each other, such as Anarchists and Communists,
helped each other out inside jail. They even edited an underground newsletter together, which was called *Bungalow*.

The old Republicans, some of them veteran Galicianists
from the Celtic Cavern and Brotherhoods of the Language,
with the air of old knights of the Round Table, who even

received Communion during Mass, acted at times as a council of elders to resolve conflicts and disputes between inmates. There were no more outings without trial. The escorts continued to do their dirty work outside, but the military had decided that a certain discipline should also prevail in the cauldrons of hell. The executions by firing squad did not stop, but the briefest of courts martial would be held first.

With this parallel administration, the prisoners did what they could to improve their situation in jail. They took the initiative on measures of hygiene and the distribution of food. Superimposed on the official timetable was an unwritten calendar, and it was this that effectively governed their daily routines. Tasks were shared out with such organization and efficiency that many ordinary prisoners came to them to ask for help. Behind bars, there was a shadow government, exactly that, a parliament and assembly, and justices of the peace. There was also a school of humanities, a tobacconist's, a joint fund acting as a mutual savings bank, and a hospital.

The prisoners' hospital was Doctor Da Barca.

"There were other staff in the infirmary," Herbal told Maria da Visitação, "but he was the one who carried the burden of responsibility. Even the official doctor, Doctor Soláns, would heed his instructions when visiting, as if he were no more than a chance auxiliary. This Soláns fellow would hardly open his mouth. We all knew he was injecting himself with some drug. You could tell he was sickened by the jail, even though he lived on the outside. He never seemed quite there, stunned by wherever in the world he had come to land in a white coat. Doctor Da Barca, however, knew all the prisoners by name and medical history, whether they were political or not, without the need for keeping records. I don't know how he did it. His head was quicker than an almanac.

"One day an official from the military health inspectorate appeared in the infirmary. He ordered a patient to be examined in his presence. Doctor Soláns was nervous, as if he felt he was being scrutinized. Doctor Da Barca meanwhile stood back, deliberately asking him for advice and handing him the initiative. Suddenly, as he bent to sit down, the official made a strange gesture and a pistol fell out of his shoulder holster. We were there to keep an eye on a prisoner considered dangerous, Genghis Khan. He had been a boxer and a wrestler, and was a bit mad and would suddenly flip. He had been jailed for unintentionally killing a man during a display of freestyle wrestling. He had meant to give him a fright, that was all. From the start of the fight between Genghis Khan and a wrestler called the Lalín Bull, this little man, who was sitting in the front row, had been shouting it was fixed. 'It's a fix! It's a fix!' Genghis Khan had blood pouring from his nostrils, he could do that, but still this repulsive little man was not satisfied, as if the spectacle of the wound confirmed his suspicions that the fight was fixed. So then Genghis Khan went berserk. He lifted the Lalín Bull, all twenty stone of him, up in the air and threw him as hard as he could on top of the man shouting that it was a fix, who never felt cheated again.

"So there we all were, in the infirmary, looking at this

pistol like it was some dead rat. And Doctor Da Barca said, calm as can be, 'My friend, your heart has fallen to the ground.' Even that big lad we had the handcuffs on, Genghis Khan, was amazed; then he burst out laughing and said, 'You got it, a bloke with three balls!' From that moment on he held Doctor Da Barca in such high esteem that he'd walk beside him in the courtyard each day as if he were covering his back and accompany him to the Latin classes given by old Carré from the Brotherhoods of the Language. Genghis Khan started using the funniest turns of phrase. He would say that such and such was *no laughing peccata* and then, when things weren't going well, *we're on the recline*. And that's how he got the name Laughing Peccata. He was well over six feet tall, though a bit bow-legged, and wore boots that were open at the front, with his toes sticking out like the roots of an oak."

In jail the prisoners also organized an orchestra. There were quite a few musicians, good musicians, the best from the Mariñas, which is where many dances were held under the Republic. Most of them were Anarchists who enjoyed romantic boleros, the melancholy of a luminous bolt of lightning. There were no instruments, but they played using their breath and hands. The trombone, saxophone and trumpet. Everyone reconstructed their instrument in the air. The percussion, however, was authentic. The one called Barbarito could play jazz on a chamber pot. There had been some discussion as to whether to call it the Ritz or Palace Orchestra, but in the end they decided on the name Five-Star.

Pepe Sánchez did the singing. He had been arrested along with dozens of other fugitives in the hold of a fishing boat, about to set course for France. Sánchez had been gifted with a voice and, when he sang in the courtyard, the inmates would gaze at the silhouette of the city – the prison was in a dip between the lighthouse and the metropolis – as if to say, "You don't know what you're missing." At times like this, any one of them would have paid to be there. In the sentry box, Herbal laid down his rifle, leant forward on the stone pillow and closed his eyes like the usher at an opera house.

There was a legend about Pepe Sánchez. On the eve of the 1936 elections, when the victory of the Left was in sight, Galicia was overrun with the so-called Missions. These were outdoor sermons, aimed primarily at the peasant women, who gave the reactionaries most of their votes. Fire-and-brimstone sermons that told of terrible plagues to come. Men and women would fornicate like beasts. The revolutionaries would separate children from their mothers as soon as they were born and educate them in atheism. They would take away their cows without paying a penny. What is more, they would carry Lenin or Bakunin in procession instead of the Virgin Mary or Holy Christ. One of these missions was due to take place in Celas and a group of Anarchists decided to break it up. They drew lots and it fell to Pepe Sánchez. This was the plan: he was to ride in on a donkey, dressed in a Dominican's habit, and interrupt the sermon in full flow like a man possessed. Pepe was far from sure about the whole idea and started the day with a pint of firewater. When he reached the place, riding the donkey, shouting "Long live Christ the King, down with Manuel Azaña!" and similar phrases, the friars who were due to give the sermon had yet to arrive, on account of some delay. So the crowd thought he was genuine and led him, protesting, towards the makeshift pulpit. Pepe Sánchez had little choice but to say a few words. So he spoke from the heart. He said that no-one in the world was sufficiently good to wield power over anyone else without their consent. That the union between man and woman had to be free, with no rings of any kind other than love and responsibility. That . . . That . . . That it's no crime to steal from a thief, and dumb is the sheep that goes to the wolf for confession. He was a handsome man, and the gale tousling his habit and romantic locks gave him the magnificent air of a prophet. After the odd initial murmur, there was silence and part of the audience, the young women in particular, began to nod their agreement and view him with devotion. And then Pepe, who was in full swing by now, as if he held the stage at the village fête, sang that bolero he liked so much.

> A girl was so brimming with happy thoughts
> she carved her name in the trunk of a tree.
> The tree was so shaken by what it saw
> it dropped a flower at the little girl's feet.

The mission was a success.

Pepe Sánchez was shot one rainy dawn in the autumn of '38. The day before, all the words disappeared from the prison. Nothing was left of them but scraps in the seagulls' scream. The lament of a bolt being drawn. The gasps of the drains. And then Pepe burst into song. He sang the whole night, accompanied from their cells by the musicians of the Five-Star Orchestra on their wind instruments. As he was taken away, with the priest behind murmuring a prayer, he had enough sense of humour to shout along the corridor, "Heaven is ours! I'm sure to get in by the eye of the needle!" He was lithe as a willow, you see.

"No, there were no volunteers for the firing squad that time," said Herbal to Maria da Visitação.

12

TWICE DOCTOR DA BARCA CONQUERED DEATH. AND twice death almost conquered him, cornering him in the cell and hurling him on to the mattress.

This occurred when Dombodán and Pepe Sánchez were shot.

"He was always in high spirits, but twice he went to pieces," Herbal told Maria da Visitação. "When The Kid and the singer died. Then, he spent various days crashed out on the mattress in a long sleep, as if he had injected himself with a barrel of valerian."

The second time he went into shock, Genghis Khan kept watch by his side.

When he woke up, he said to him, "What are you doing here, LP?"

"Getting rid of the lice, doctor. And keeping the rats at bay."

"Have I slept for so long?"

"Three days and three nights."

"Thank you, Genghis. I'm going to buy you lunch."

"And you see," Herbal told Maria da Visitação, "he had the power of the look."

At lunchtime, in the dining hall, Doctor Da Barca and Genghis Khan sat down opposite one another and all the prisoners were astonished witnesses of that banquet.

"You're going to start with a seafood cocktail. Lobster with mayonnaise, served on a heart of lettuce from the Barcia Valley."

"And to drink?" Genghis Khan asked incredulously.

"To drink," Doctor Da Barca said very seriously, "a white Rosal."

He was staring at him, drawing him into his eyes, and something was happening because Genghis Khan stopped laughing, hesitated for a moment as if he were at a height and suffering vertigo, and then fell into a daze. Doctor Da Barca stood up, went around the table and gently closed his eyelids as if they were lace curtains.

"Is the cocktail good?"

Genghis Khan nodded with his mouth full.

"And the wine?"

"Ju . . . just right," he stammered ecstatically.

"Well, take it slowly."

Afterwards, when Doctor Da Barca served him a main course of rump steak and creamed potatoes, washed down with a red Amandi, Genghis Khan slowly changed colour. The pale, lean giant exhibited now the healthy glow of a gluttonous abbot. He gleamed with expansive, country abundance, in a sweet revenge on time, affecting everyone present.

A hush of tongues on palates and fabled eyes fell over the dining hall, silencing the stirring of spoons during the meal, an unfathomable soup they called *water for washing meat*.

"Now, Genghis," Doctor Da Barca said solemnly, "the promised dessert."

"Treacle tart!" someone shouted out, unable to repress their anxiety.

"*Millefeuille!*"

"Almond cake!"

A cloud of icing sugar swept across the dark hall. Meringue bubbled up in the draught from the doors. Honey oozed down the bare walls.

Doctor Da Barca gestured with his hands for silence.

"Chestnuts, Genghis," he said at last. There followed the murmur of disconcerted voices, because that was the kind of rubbish poor people ate.

"Look, Genghis, chestnuts from the Courel Mountains, from the land of chestnut groves, boiled in calamint and fennel. You're a child, Genghis, the dogs howl in the wind, the night trembles in the oil lamp and the adults stoop under the weight of winter. But there's your mother, Genghis, placing the dish of boiled chestnuts on the middle of the table, young creatures swathed in warm rags, the waft of an animal that softens the bones. It's the incense of the earth, Genghis, can't you tell?"

And of course he could tell. The spell's fumes took hold of his senses like tendrils of ivy, stung him in the eyes and made him cry.

"And now, Genghis," said Doctor Da Barca, switching tone like an actor, "let us pour chocolate sauce over those chestnuts, in the French style, yes, indeed."

Everyone approved this daintiness.

In the report detailing anything untoward in the dining hall, the prison governor read, "The inmates refused lunch today, showing no sign of protest and giving no reason for their attitude. The withdrawal from the hall passed off without incident."

"Does he not look well?" Doctor Da Barca said. "You see, it's true what they say, you can feed off the fantasy as well. It's the fantasy that raises his glucose."

Genghis Khan came out of hypnosis, woken by his own belch of pleasure.

13

ON OCCASION THE DECEASED WOULD DISMOUNT from the saddle behind his ear, leave the guard's head and not return for some time. "He'll be out there somewhere, looking for his son," Herbal would think with a touch of nostalgia, because, after all, it was the painter who kept him company during the hours he was on duty, the nights he was on watch. Not only that, he taught him things. For example, that nothing was more difficult to paint than snow. And fields and the sea. Wide, open surfaces that give the impression of being monochrome. "Eskimos," the painter told him, "distinguish up to forty colours in snow, forty types of whiteness. That is why the best person to paint the sea, fields and snow is a child. Then the snow can be green and the field grow white like a peasant farmer in old age."

"Have you ever painted snow?"

"I did once, for the theatre. A stage-set of werewolves. If you put a wolf in the middle, it's a lot easier. A black wolf, like a piece of smouldering wood in the distance, and at most a bare beech tree painted on to a sheet. Then all you need is for someone to say snow. The theatre is wonderful."

"It seems strange to hear you say that," said the guard, scratching his tangled beard with the front sight of his rifle.

"Why?"

"I thought for you, as a painter, images were more important than words."

"What is important is to see, that is what is important. In fact," the painter added, "Homer, the first writer, is reputed to have been blind."

"Which means," the guard remarked with a touch of sarcasm, "that he must have had very good eyesight."

"Exactly. That's exactly what it means."

The two of them fell silent, drawn by the sun setting on the stage. It slid behind Mount San Pedro on its way to a quay of exile. On the other side of the bay, the first watercolours from the lighthouse intensified the sea's ballad.

"Shortly before dying," the painter said, and he said it as if the fact of having died were alien to them both, "I painted this very scene, the one we are seeing now. It was part of the set design for *Canto Mariñán* sung by the Ruada Choir at the Theatre Rosalía de Castro."

"I'd like to have seen it," said the guard with heartfelt politeness.

"It was nothing out of this world. What suggested the sea was the lighthouse, Hercules Tower. The sea was the shadows. I didn't want to paint it. I wanted it to be heard like a litany. The sea is impossible to paint. A painter in his right mind, for all the realism he would like to introduce, knows that you cannot transfer the sea on to a canvas. There was one, an Englishman – Turner he was called – who did it very well. His shipwreck of a slave traders' boat is the most astonishing image of the sea that exists. In it, you can hear the sea. In the shout of the slaves. Slaves who possibly knew no more about the sea than the rolling of the hold. I should like to paint the sea from within, but not having drowned, in a diving suit. To go down with a canvas, paintbrushes and the rest, as I'm told a Japanese painter did.

"I have a friend who might do this," he added with a nostalgic smile. "That's if he does not drown in wine first. His name is Lugrís."

Dusk, for some reason, was when the painter preferred to visit the guard Herbal's head. He would alight on his ear with firm gentleness, with one leg on either side, like the carpenter's pencil.

When he felt the pencil, when they spoke of these things – of the colours of snow, of the scythe of the paintbrush on the green silence of the meadows, of the underwater painter, of a railwayman's lantern breaking through the night mist or of a glow-worm's phosphorescence – the guard Herbal noticed how the feeling of breathlessness would disappear, as if by magic, the bubbling of his lungs like a pair of moist bellows, the delirium and cold sweat that followed the nightmare of an explosion in his temple. The guard Herbal felt good being what he was then, a forgotten man in his sentry box. He managed to keep his heart in time to the stonemason's chisel, so that it beat with a minimum routine. Thinking was the luminous projector in a cinema. As when he was a shepherd boy, and his gaze held a goldcrest pecking the profile of time on the bark's vertical line or kept a blade of grass on the edge of the eddy's fatal clock in the fountain.

"Look, the washerwomen are painting the hillside," the dead man was telling him now.

Over the thickets around the Lighthouse, between the rocky outcrops, two washerwomen were hanging out the clothes to dry. Their load was like a magician's cloth stomach. From it, they produced endless coloured articles that repainted the hillside. Their plump, rosy hands obeyed the guard's eyes, eyes that in turn were guided by the painter, "Washerwomen have pink hands because they scrub so much on the stone in the water that the years are lifted from their skin. Their hands are the hands they had when they were girls and first became washerwomen.

"Their arms," the painter added, "are the handles of a paintbrush, coloured like alder wood, because they also formed by the side of the river. When they wring out the wet clothes, the washerwomen's arms tense like roots along a riverbank. The hillside is like a canvas. Look. They are painting over gorse bushes and brambles. The prickles are the best pegs the washerwoman has. There she goes. The long brush stroke of a white sheet. Two dashes of red socks. The slight tremor of some lingerie. Hanging out to dry, each article of clothing tells a story.

"Washerwomen's hands have hardly any nails. This also tells a story, as, if we had an X-ray, would the spine's upper vertebrae, deformed by the weight of the loads piled on to their heads over the years. Washerwomen have hardly any nails. The salamander is said to have stolen them with its breath. But that, as far as it goes, is a magical explanation. Their nails were consumed by caustic soda."

In the dead man's absence, the Iron Man strove to take his place in the guard Herbal's head. The Iron Man would show up not at a lazy, melancholy time such as twilight, nor in order to settle himself like a carpenter's pencil on the saddle behind his ear, but first thing in the morning, in the mirror, when he was shaving. Herbal did not find waking up easy. He spent the whole night panting, like someone climbing up and down mountains pulling at a mule laden with corpses. So the Iron Man found him more than receptive to pieces of advice that were really commands. "Learn to hold your gaze and use it to dominate. That is why you should clench your teeth. Open your mouth as little as possible. Words, however imperious and rude, always represent an open door to dilettantes, and the weakest grab on to them as a ship-wrecked sailor clings to a mast. Silence, accompanied by martial, categorical gestures, has the effect of intimidation. Human relationships, do not forget, are always established in terms of power. As with wolves, exploratory contact leads to a new order: dominance or submission. And button up that trench coat, soldier! You're a winner. Let them know it."

In the room his sister had given him, there was a bicycle

hanging on the wall. It was a bicycle that no-one used, the tyres so clean they looked as if they had never been placed on the ground. The tin mudguards gleamed like sheets of German silver. Before going to sleep, he would sit on the bed in front of the bicycle. As a child he had dreamt of something similar. Or had he? Perhaps it was a dream he dreamt he had dreamed. Suddenly, he felt cheated. All he could remember having dreamt, the dream that displaced all his dreams, was that girl, that young woman, that woman, called Marisa Mallo. There she was, on the wall, like a statue of the Blessed Virgin on the altar.

Grazing the cattle, he would often run off with his uncle the trapper. But he had another uncle. Another loner. Nan, his carpenter uncle.

When he returned with the cows, he would stop off at Nan's workshop, a shed that gave on to the road, made of planks coated with pitch, like a grounded ark at the entrance to the village. To Herbal, Nan was a strange creature. There was in the orchard an apple tree covered with moss, the blackbirds' favourite. It was the same, in his family, with that carpenter great-uncle. Old age was on the lookout in the village. Suddenly, it would fling teeth into a dark corner, cloak the women in mourning in a misty side street, change voices with a swig of firewater, and wrinkle skin in the stepping stone of a winter. But old age had not pierced Nan. It had fallen over him, covered him in white hair, tufts that curled on his chest and clothed his arms the way the moss clothed the apple tree's branches, but his skin shone yellow like the heart of a local pine, his teeth sparkled with good humour, and then he always carried that red plume behind his ear. The carpenter's pencil. It was never cold in Nan's workshop. The ground was a soft bed of shavings. The aroma of sawdust soaked up the humidity. "Where've you been?" he would ask, knowing full well. "A kid like you should be at school." And then he would murmur with a disapproving gesture, "They cut the wood too soon. Come here, Herbal. Close your eyes. Now tell me, just by the smell, as I taught you, which is chestnut and which is birch?" The child sniffed in the air, bringing his nose closer until the tip was brushing the pieces of wood. "Not like that. Do it without touching. Just by using the smell."

"This one's birch," Herbal pointed finally with his finger.

"Are you sure?"

"I'm sure."

"What makes you say that?"

"It smells of woman."

"Very good, Herbal."

And then he would draw the stump of birch towards him and breathe in deeply, half-closing his eyes. Woman bathed in the river.

Herbal takes the bicycle down from the wall. The handlebars and mudguards gleam like German silver. Underneath the bed is Nan's box of tools, which he ties to the rack. He makes some coffee in the pot, like an infusion, the way Nan would. It is dawn outside and he starts pedalling along the road that follows the river, bordered by birch trees. A strange figure is coming the other way. It is wearing a robe and is so made up it looks like a mask. It gestures to him to stop. Herbal tries to pedal harder but the chain comes off the sprocket.

"Hello, Herbal, dear. I am Death. Do you know where a smiling young accordionist and that slut, Life, might be?"

But then Herbal, searching for a weapon, something with which to defend himself, grabs hold of the pencil behind his ear. It grows to the length of a red spear. The graphite at the end glitters like polished metal. Death opens her eyes in horror. She vanishes. All that is left is a petrol stain in a puddle on the road. Herbal repairs the bike and pedals along, happily whistling a goldfinch's paso doble, with the red pencil behind his ear. He arrives at Marisa Mallo's house in the country and greets her cheerfully, looking up at the sky. "Lovely day!" "Beautiful," she agrees. "Right," he says, rubbing his hands together, "what'll it be today?" "A trough, Herbal. A kneading trough."

"Fashioned out of walnut, my lady. With the legs nicely turned and an escutcheon on the keyhole."

"And a cabinet, Herbal. Will you make me a cabinet as well?"

"With a baluster of scrolls."

He woke up to the Iron Man's orders. He had fallen asleep on top of the bed, fully clothed. In the kitchen he could hear his sister's docile screams. He recalled what Sergeant Landesa had told him. "Give him a kick in the balls from me." "That's enough," he murmured. "The bastard."

"Did you catch that? I want a hot plate of food waiting

for me on the table. And I don't care what time it is!"

His sister was in a nightdress, her hair dishevelled, carrying a bowl of soup in her hands. Herbal's presence seemed to startle her further because she spilled part of the bowl. The husband was wearing uniform. The blue shirt. The leather straps. The pistol in its shoulder holster. He stared at him. Through stretch-marked eyes. Drunk. He gave the hint of a cynical smile. Then he wiped his tongue over his teeth.

"Can you not sleep, Herbal?"

He took out the pistol and placed it on the table. Next to the cutlery and piece of bread, the Star resembled some absurd, helpless tool. Zalo Puga filled two glasses with wine.

"Hey, come and sit down. Have a drink with your brother-in-law. You," he addressed his wife, "can put that away."

He winked at Herbal and began to slurp straight from the bowl. He was always like this. He would swing from aggressive arrogance to drunken camaraderie. Beatriz attempted to hide the marks of ill-treatment, but sometimes, when they were alone, she would break down and cry in her brother's arms. Now, having untied the sack her husband had brought home with him, Herbal saw how she was taken aback and shuddered, as if she might fall.

"Well, what do you think? A good day's hunting! Go on then, get it out."

"I'd rather do it tomorrow."

"Come on, woman. It won't bite. Let your brother see."

Overcoming her disgust, she put her hands in and finally pulled out a pig's head. She turned it around to face the men, holding it as far away as possible. Grains of salt in the oblique hollows of its eyes.

"Poor thing!"

Herbal's brother-in-law laughed at his own joke. "It's all there, the tail and everything!" Then he added, "The stupid old woman didn't want to let it go. She said she'd already given a son for Franco. Ha, ha, ha!"

Zalo Puga had put on a lot of weight since the start of the war. He worked in Supplies. He would go around the different villages in the company of others, confiscating foodstuffs. And keep a part of the booty for himself. "She didn't want to let it go," he said again in a sordid tone. "She clung on to the hams like relics. I had to shake her loose."

When Beatriz dragged the sack out to the pantry, he produced two cigars from his shirt pocket and offered one to Herbal. The first wisps of smoke crossed and ascended, locked in a struggle, towards the lamp. Zalo Puga stared at him through the stretch marks in his eyes.

"You'd like to kill me, wouldn't you? But you don't have the balls."

And he burst out laughing for a second time.

14

IN BETWEEN THE PRISON AND THE FIRST HOUSES of the city were some high cliffs. Sometimes, when the men were taking their break in the courtyard, women would appear on the cliffs' summit, seemingly sculpted but for the sea breeze that ruffled their skirts and long hair. In the sunny corner of the courtyard, some of the men would shield their eyes from the sun and gaze at them. They made no gesture. Only once in a while would the women slowly wave their arms, as with a flag code that grows more agitated the moment it is recognized.

From the sentry box in a corner of the prison wall, with the carpenter's pencil behind his ear, Herbal listened to what the painter was telling him.

He was telling him that beings and things are clothed in light. That even the Gospels talk of men as "the children of light". Between the prisoners in the courtyard and the women on the cliffs, there had to be threads of light running over the wall, invisible threads that would however transmit the colour of clothing and the trousseau of memory. And not just that, a gangway of luminous and sensory ropes. The guard imagined that, still as they were, the prisoners and the women on the cliffs were making love and it was the gale of their fingers tossing their skirts and long hair.

One day he saw her among the other women wearing shabby clothes. Her long, russet hair stirred by the breeze, laying threads to the doctor in the prison courtyard. Silk threads, invisible threads. Not even an accurate marksman would know how to tear them.

Today there were no women. A group of children with shaved heads, making them look like small men, were playing soldiers with sticks instead of swords. They were fighting for the top of the cliffs like the towers of a fort. They tired of fencing, and started using the same sticks as rifles. They would fall down dead and roll over, like extras in a film, and then stand up laughing and again roll down the hillside until they were close to the prison wall. One of them, having fallen, raised his eyes and met the guard's gaze. He picked up the stick, rested it against his shoulder, with one foot forward in a marksman's stance, and aimed at him. "Brat," said the guard. And he decided to give him a fright. He picked up his rifle and aimed in turn in the kid's direction. The others were stunned and shouted out to him from behind. "Run, Chip! Run!" The boy slowly lowered his stick weapon. He had a freckled face and a bold, toothless grin. Suddenly, in one swift movement, he placed the stick back against his shoulder, shot – bang, bang! – and took to his heels, pulling himself up the hillside in his patchwork trousers. The guard followed him with the front sight of his rifle. Herbal could feel his cheeks burning. When the boy disappeared behind the cliffs, he laid down the weapon and breathed deeply. He was short of breath. The sweat was pouring off him. He heard the echo of a guffaw. The Iron Man had caused the painter to dismount. The Iron Man was laughing at him.

"What's that you're carrying behind your ear?"

"A pencil. A carpenter's pencil. It's a way of remembering someone I killed."

"That's quite some booty!"

On 1 April 1939, Franco signed the victory dispatch.

"Today we are celebrating the victory of God," said the chaplain in his homily during the High Mass held in the courtyard. He did not say it with any great haughtiness, rather as someone who is stating the law of gravity. That day, guards had been placed in between the rows of prisoners. Authorities were in attendance and the governor did not want unpleasant surprises, insurrections of laughter or coughing, as had happened on previous occasions when some preacher had rubbed salt into the wound, blessed the war he called a Crusade and urged them to repent, fallen angels of the band of Beelzebub, and to ask for divine protection for General Franco. The chaplain, however, was different, his fanaticism less prosaic. It had a certain theological framework, which he had worked on in discussions with the inmates, most of whom were fanatical readers. They would read anything they could lay their hands on, be it *Bibliotheca Sanctorum* or

Wonders of Insect Life. The Curia would have envied them such knowledge! They knew Latin, God, they knew Greek. Like that Doctor Da Barca fellow, who one day embroiled him in a spider's web of soma, psyche and pneuma.

"*Pneuma tes aletheias.* The Spirit of Truth. You know? That is what the Holy Spirit means. Of Truth, Father."

"God does not go into battle against men for the sake of it," the chaplain said. "No creature is an enemy in God's eyes. It is sin, the manifestation of Satan, that angers God. Besides, who are we from his heights? Small pinheads. What God does is guide the waters of history, in the same way that the miller governs the river's course. God wages war against sin, not against venial sins, which we are left to handle by means of confession, repentance and forgiveness. First of all there is original sin, *peccatum originale*, the stigma we bear for having been born. Then there are the venial sins (or veritable sins!) of the person per se, *peccatum personale*, those slip-ups along the way. But the worst of them all, the one that hovers over us and possessed a part of Spain in recent years, betraying her essential being, is the Sin of History. Sin with a capital S. This terribly pernicious caste of Sin takes root above all in the vanity of intellect, in the ignorance of simpler folk, who are swept along by temptations in the form of revolutions and ludicrous social Utopias. Against this Sin of History, God will wage war. And, as the Scriptures clearly tell us, the wrath of God exists, a wrath that is just and implacable. God chooses the instruments of his victory. God's chosen ones."

The chaplain read out the telegram that Pope Pius XII had sent Franco on 31 March, "Lifting up our hearts to God, we give sincere thanks to His Excellency for the victory of Catholic Spain."

At this point someone cleared their throat.

"It was Doctor Da Barca," Herbal told Maria da Visitação. "I know because I was standing next to him and gave him a hard stare, calling him to order. We were under instructions to quell any incident. But aside from staring at him like something the cat brought in, which he really didn't care about, there wasn't much I could do. He had a dry, artificial cough, the cough of refined people who go to concerts. I was almost relieved when the cough spread like a disease among all the prisoners. It sounded like a huge carillon peeling off the bell tower.

"We didn't know what to do. We could hardly lay into them all in the middle of Mass. The authorities stirred uneasily in their seats. Deep down, we were all hoping the chaplain, in other respects no fool, would quash the rebellious murmur with a timely silence. But, like a cogged wheel engaging with another, bigger wheel, he was inflamed with the gears of his own sermon."

"The wrath of God exists! It was God's victory!"

His voice was drowned out by the coughing, no longer the delicate clearing of the throat at the opera but the undertow of a surging sea. The prison governor, assailed by looks from the authorities, decided to go over to him and mutter in his ear that he should cut it short, today was Victory

84

Day and if things carried on as they were they would be celebrating it with a massacre.

The chaplain's flushed face turned pale, undone by the frenzy of men coughing as if with silicosis. He went quiet, scanned the rows with disconcerted eyes, as if coming to, and mumbled some Latin under his breath.

What the chaplain said, and Herbal would be unable to remember, was, "Ubi est mors stimulus tuus?"

At the end of the ceremony, the governor gave the cries that were de rigueur.

"Spain!" Only the voices of the authorities and guards were heard, "One!"

"Spain!" The prisoners remained silent. The same voices cried, "Great!"

"Spain!" And then the whole prison thundered, "Free!"

Herbal had found out about the victory a long time before from the defeated. "Contrary to what people think," he said to Maria da Visitação, "prison is a good place to receive information. The news you get from the conquered is often the most reliable." Barcelona fell in January, Madrid fell in March. Toledo fell on the first of April, April showers. Every time a city fell you could see it on their faces like a wrinkle, a circle of shade around their sunken eyes, you could see it in their languid walk, their neglected appearance. Bombarded with bad news, the inmates bore the fatigue of a defeated column down corridors and in the courtyard. And with renewed force, like a virus lurking in the miasma, the ailments and epidemics returned.

Doctor Da Barca continued to shave every day. He would wash methodically at the washstand using a small mirror with a crack that split his face in two. He regularly combed his hair as for a feast day. And cleaned his worn-out shoes, which had the sheen of a sepia photograph. He attended to such details as a chess player attends to his pawns. He had asked Marisa for a photograph. Then he had thought better of it.

"Take it, it wasn't a good idea."

She seemed offended. No-one likes being given back a photograph, especially in prison.

"I don't want to see you stuck between four walls. Give me something of yours. Something I can use to go to sleep."

She was wearing a scarf tied in a knot around her neck. She held it out to him. Never less than a yard apart. Forbidden to touch.

Herbal intervened. He inspected it with apparent indifference. Made of cotton with a red frill. How he would have liked to inhale the scent! "Red is not allowed," he said, which was true, but he dropped it into Marisa's hands.

"I'm leaving," the deceased told Herbal shortly after the end of the war. "I'm going to see if I can find my son. You wouldn't happen to know anything, would you?"

"He's alive, I told you so," replied the guard, somewhat annoyed. "When we went to find him, he'd left. We later learnt he'd dressed up as a blind man and boarded a coach. Even with a blind man's glasses, he must have seen the corpses in the ditches at the side of the road. We lost track of him here, in Coruña."

"Well, I'm going to see if I can find him. I'd promised to teach him how to paint."

"I don't suppose he'll be up to much painting," the guard remarked crudely. "He'll be living like a mole."

From the moment the painter left, and as he feared, Herbal noticed the sense of unease return. Unable to face up to his brother-in-law, he left his sister's house and asked for authorization to spend nights at the prison. In the morning, when he stood up, he felt giddy, as if his head were unwilling to get up with his body. He was not looking well.

That Doctor Da Barca fellow got on his nerves. His sprightly bearing. His serenity. His Daniel's smile.

The Iron Man made the most of the painter's absence. Herbal listened to what he had to say.

He reported Doctor Da Barca. He reported him for something he had known for quite some time.

The doctor had a secret radio. The parts had been smuggled in from the outside, hidden in jars from the infirmary. The aerial was the metal sprung base of a bed. The prisoners' organization had arranged shifts of patients needing urgent attention as a way of covering up the traffic in and out of the infirmary at night. He had caught the doctor with the headphones. The doctor had tried telling him sardonically it was a stethoscope, but he was not stupid.

He reported him for something else. He had very serious suspicions. Doctor Da Barca was administering drugs to some of the sick.

"One night," Herbal explained to the governor, "we took

an inmate to the infirmary complaining of sharp pains. He was shouting like someone was sawing at his bones. And in fact, in between screams, he said his right foot really hurt. But the funny thing is the patient, by the name of Biqueira, didn't have a right foot. It had been amputated some months previously for gangrene. He was one of those who tried to get away, sir, if you recall, when they were painting the front of the prison. It was me who shot him in the ankle. Messed it all up. 'It must be the other foot,' I told him, 'the left foot.' But no, he said it was the right foot and clung with desperation, sticking in his nails, to the thigh on that side. He had a wooden leg, a walnut leg they had made for him in the workshop. 'It must be the wood not fitting the stump.' And I removed the leg, but he said, 'It's the foot, idiot, the bullet in my ankle.' So we took him to the infirmary and Doctor Da Barca said very seriously that it was the foot, the right foot at the ankle. That the bullet was giving him pain. It struck me by now they were putting it on. Then the doctor gave him an injection before my eyes, saying it would make him better. 'It's all right, Biqueira. It's the sleep of Morpheus.' Almost immediately Biqueira went quiet and a happy look came over his face, as if he were daydreaming. I asked the doctor what had happened, but he didn't bother to reply. He's a stuck-up customer. He doesn't even deign to address me. I heard him explaining to the others that what Biqueira had was a phantom pain."

"And what else?" the governor frowned.

"It happened again, sir. I discovered they were stealing

morphine from Doctor Solán's safety cabinet."

"I have heard nothing about that cabinet being broken into."

The last remark struck Herbal as exceptionally naive. He said, "There are a dozen thieves in this prison, sir, able to open that cabinet in a flash using a toothpick. You can be sure they pay more attention to the doctor than to you or me." And then he calmly produced a parcel wrapped in brown paper. "They're open phials, sir, recovered from the rubbish in the infirmary. I took it upon myself to find out that they contained morphine."

The governor scrutinized this vocational justiciary who had turned up in his office, as if discovering for the first time that he was at his service. He thought of a dog trailing a string of cans tied to its tail, causing an almighty racket.

"Doctor Solán's has had no complaint."

"He'll have his reasons," Herbal said, holding his gaze.

"I appreciate your professionalism, officer." He stood up. The conversation was at an end. "Leave this to me."

Herbal kept an eye on events. Doctor Da Barca was held in solitary confinement for a time, on account of the confiscated radio. Doctor Soláns was off sick for a long period. As for him, he was notified one day of his promotion to corporal.

He felt worse and worse. He would vent his anger on the prisoners and soon became especially hated. He would deliberately do bad things. One day he told Ventura, a young lad who was a fisherman, "Go to the watchtower this afternoon. I'll let you see into the women's courtyard. We've a new little slut who's got two tits like Arzúa cheeses. If you signal to her, she'll show you the lot." "But we're not allowed up there," said the inmate. "I'll pretend not to notice," replied Herbal.

At the time of the military coup, Ventura had been playing a conch shell day and night in Coruña Bay until they silenced him with a gunshot. The bullet pierced his forearm, as if they had deliberately aimed at a tattoo there of an opulent mermaid, which was now deformed by the scar.

At the agreed hour, Ventura climbed up the tower. There was only one young girl in the courtyard, squatting against the wall. The young inmate whistled and signalled with his arm. The girl struggled to her feet and made her way awkwardly towards the middle of the courtyard, as if she were on stilts. She was wearing an old fur-lined coat and blue wellington boots. She looked up and Ventura thought she had the saddest eyes he had ever seen. She was blonde, her face was swollen, and deep bags coloured like tortoiseshell arched below her eyes. Suddenly, she opened her coat. She was naked underneath. She opened and closed it, as if performing in a marquee at the fairground. The girl had two shrunken tits, hair on her chest, and a penis. "What are you doing here?" Herbal asked, "don't you know you're not allowed?"

"You're a bastard."

"Ha, ha, ha!"

Every day he would stop by at the punishment cell where Doctor Da Barca was and spit through the small window in the door. One night he woke up, gasping for breath. His heart was thrashing inside his chest. He was so frightened he could not get back to sleep and went to the punishment cell where Da Barca was sleeping, leant panting beside the door and was on the verge of asking for help. In the end, he went out into the fresh air of the courtyard and began to breathe deeply.

It was then he noticed the deceased settling himself behind his ear. A miraculous relief.

"Is that you? Where the hell have you been?" he asked, concealing his delight. "Did you find your son?"

"No, I didn't. But I heard the family say he was safe."

"I told you so. You should trust me."

"Should I now?" the dead man replied ironically.

"Listen, painter. Tell me something. Do you know what phantom pain is?"

"I've heard of it. Daniel Da Barca explained it to me once. He carried out a study for Local Welfare. Apparently it's the worst pain you can get, a pain that becomes unbearable. The memory of pain. The pain of what you have lost. Why do you ask?"

"No reason."

15

MARISA MALLO LOOKED IN THE DIRECTION OF THE monkey puzzle and felt, in turn, the weight of another's eyes. That majestic specimen planted in the ground of her grandfather's country home dominated the valley and reached the sky with its huge, vegetal steps.

The dogs had come out to welcome her. They recognized her smell and fought over it with savage delight. In leaps and bounds, they showed off the visitor, like a precious conquest. But Marisa had never felt that other sensation, of being spied on by the monkey puzzle.

"So you're back again, are you, girl?" it said to her from on high.

As she made her way towards the house, she felt the trees in blossom were scrutinizing her as well, next to the path of white pebbles. As if the camellias were giving each other a nudge and the Chinese magnolias were whispering gently.

Somehow that world belonged to her. It had been both her playground and hideaway. There, something her grandfather had particularly wanted, she had made her debut in society with an exotic party in the Fronteira tradition. She laughed with ironic melancholy just to remember it.

Her grandfather, Benito Mallo, sat with her by his side beneath the vine arbour, presiding at the long banquet table. So long in her mind's eye that the white of the tablecloths merged at the edges with the foliage of the garden. Next to his grandchild, that red-haired girl already blossoming into a beautiful woman, Benito Mallo smiled with satisfaction. It was the first time he had managed to assemble all the so-called bigwigs. There, in pride of place, were the people who despised him most, the town's top pedigree, meekly rendering thanks. There were the bishop and the priests, including the parish priest who had singled him out from the pulpit one day as the captain of sinners. There were the border-guard chiefs, the very ones who had sworn when he was an audacious nobody to hang him upside down from the bridge, so that the eels could pick out his eyes. But something had happened to reality. It was still the same. The same values, the same laws, the same God. Only that Benito Mallo had crossed the border, had got rich from smuggling. Coffee, oil and *bacalao* were talked about. But the popular imagination knew more: the tons of copper amassed by means of electric cables that terminated in a handle turning day and night; the jewellery that came across in the cattle's stomachs; the silk carried by a legion of falsely-pregnant women; the weapons bestowing honours on a dead man in a coffin.

Benito Mallo had attained that level of wealth at which

people stop asking where it has come from. He had forged a legend. The country boy who wore cut suits made in Coruña. Who bought a Ford with leather-covered seats where the hens laid their clutches. Who had taps made of gold but went to the toilet on the hillside and cleaned himself with cabbage leaves. Who gave his lovers fake banknotes.

Some of this changed when Benito Mallo bought the manor house with the large araucaria. An unwritten rule said that whoever owned the monkey-puzzle owned the mayorship. And one of Benito Mallo's trusted lawyers was appointed mayor during Primo de Rivera's dictatorship. This did not mean that the invisible border kingdom ceased to function. Benito Mallo wove a firm tapestry with the shuttle of day and night. He stepped with confidence into the carpeted drawing-rooms, made the haughtiest of civil servants and judges diligent, but, sometimes, at night, you might spot him on a wharf beside the Miño, in his unmistakable wide-brimmed hat, telling whoever wanted to see him here I am, the king of the river. And then, spitting on the ground in a bar, he would be celebrating the unloading of some goods. "Those months I was away, I was in New York, you know? I bought this suit and a gas station on 42nd Street." And his men knew that it might not be a bluff. "That's great, boss, just like Al Capone." They would laugh when he laughed. He had a very good sense of humour, but it would depend. When he was angered, you could see the bottom of his eyes, the flames of an oven. "That Al Capone is a criminal. I'm not." "Of course, Don Benito. Forgive the joke."

Benito Mallo read with some difficulty. "I never had an education," he would say. This declaration of ignorance sounded like a warning on his lips, which became more emphatic the more his position improved. The only papers he considered to be of any value were the deeds to property. He would read them aloud, very slowly, almost spelling out the words, unconcerned by the show of stupidity, as if they were verses from the Bible. And then he would sign with a kind of ink stab.

In order to buy the manor in Fronteira, Benito Mallo had first had to overcome the qualms of the heirs to the estate. They were based in Madrid and only visited in the summer holidays and at Christmas. At Christmas they would mount a living crib. The poor children of the parish would play the figures in the stable, except for the Virgin Mary and Joseph, who were played by the family's two children. It was they who at the end of the function handed around a Christmas box containing chocolate and dried figs. On one occasion Benito Mallo had taken the part of a shepherd, with a fur waistcoat and bag. He carried a lamb in his arms, which he had to place as an offering before the Virgin Mary, Joseph and the baby Jesus. The child in the cradle that year was a maidservant's, a son from behind the bushes. Rumour had it in Fronteira that the father was Luís Felipe, the lord of the manor. Benito Mallo was an illegitimate child as well, but he already knew who his father had been: a reckless man who organized firework displays and was stabbed to death at a village fête. Years later, when he was a young man on the brink of fame,

Benito Mallo had burst in drunk, on horseback, during the local festivities, and broken up the dance firing shots into the air. Everyone remembered the words he had shouted with resentful melancholy, before disappearing into the funnel of night.

"At the village fête, my father died!"

In the crib in the manor chapel, in his role as a shepherd, he had to sing a short carol. The night before, his mother taught him some verses, which made him crease with laughter. After placing the lamb at the foot of the cradle with the baby Jesus, Benito Mallo stepped towards the audience and, looking deadly serious, came out with the song.

> *For our Christmas box*
> *we don't want a lot:*
> *a rasher of bacon*
> *and a half on top.*

The lord and lady of the manor and their friends were initially stunned into silence. Then they burst out laughing. An unending guffaw. Benito Mallo saw how some of them wiped away the tears. They were crying with laughter. He could feel the burning in the bottom of his eyes. Had it been night, they would have glinted like the eyes of a wild cat.

The intermediaries Benito Mallo sent to Madrid were having no success. It was like hammering at cold iron. The family, who had come down in the world, would set new conditions each time the deal was virtually closed. One day Benito Mallo called for his chauffeur and told him to prepare for a long journey. They loaded two drums into the boot, of the sort used for packing smoke-dried fish. "I have brought this for his lordship and her ladyship," he said on arrival at the flat in Madrid. "Tell them it is from Benito Mallo." He was shown into the drawing-room and opened the first drum there and then, in the presence of the family, without further ado. The notes were carefully stacked in concentric circles, like slim herrings. Appetizing. See how they shine and smell. Go ahead. Try them. Chew them. Tasty, smoked fish. But what Benito Mallo said was, "Go ahead. Count them. Take your time." He looked at his pocket watch. "I have to buy a lottery ticket. If you're in agreement, I suggest you call a notary, one you trust." But when he came back, the sardonic smile on the lord's face was more pronounced. The wife remained speechless, unable to contain her breathing. The two children, boy and girl, flanked their father. Craning their necks, on the lookout, as if witnessing an affront.

"So . . ."

"We appreciate your interest," said Luís Felipe, "but it all seems so sudden. It's not just a question of money, Mr Mallo. Certain things you can't put a price on, things with strong sentimental value."

"The library, daddy," the daughter prompted.

"Yes. Take the library, for instance. It is an extraordinary library. One of the best in Galicia. Its value is incalculable."

"I see. Couto," Benito Mallo turned to the chauffeur, "bring up another drum of fish."

It would be years before Benito Mallo paid any more

attention to that library, which lined the walls of the study, the drawing-room and a long corridor of the house. Once in a while a visitor would make some admiring comment, after leafing through the old volumes.

"What you've got here is amazing, a real treasure."

"I know," Benito Mallo would proudly agree. "Its value is incalculable."

At the far end of the study that he used as an office was an illustrated encyclopaedia. The solid, symmetrical volumes looked as if they were bound in marble and gave the room the heavy air of a mausoleum. But whenever he stood up from his chair and went to the right of the table, the old smuggler would find himself at eye level before a worrying shelf of uneven books, some of them without their binding, under an epigraph of letters carved in wood:

Poetry

One day he stood up and sat down again. In his hands he had a book entitled *The One Hundred Best Spanish Poems* by Don Marcelino Menéndez y Pelayo. From then on, he would devote a little leisure time every day to reading that book. Sometimes he would leave it open in his lap and deep in thought gaze at the film the sky was projecting on the balcony or close his eyes in a daydream. He gave the servants instructions that he should not be disturbed, and they invented a new expression, as if this were an age-old custom, "His lordship is with the book."

The grandfather's obsessions were sacred and no-one had given too much thought to this sudden interest, ascribing it to the softening of the head that comes with age. But one day he took a step forward, appeared before his family, in the dining room, and recited the first stanza of Jorge Manrique's *Coplas* on the death of his father. The effect it had, grandmother Leonor's emotion and the others' astonished expressions, opened the door to a dimension of human triumph that he had not known existed. Benito Mallo had a problem, however. He was so practically minded that he confused the conclusions he came to, even those that were false, with the natural order of life.

On the day Marisa made her debut, when the banquet had been cleared away, her grandfather stood up and with his teaspoon clinked a glass like a bell calling for silence. He had spent the night before shut up in the study, and had been heard talking to himself and declaiming in different registers. Here was a man who despised speeches. Actions speak louder than words. "And yet today," he said, "I wanted to say something straight from the heart, like water rising at the soul's source. And what better opportunity than this festive occasion on which we celebrate, not without nostalgia, the spring of life, the flower's awakening, the passage from innocence to Cupid's sweet arrows?"

One or two people cleared their throat and Benito Mallo silenced them with a glare out of the corner of his eye.

"I know that many of you will be surprised by these words, and even I am not above the mockery more sentimental feelings receive in this day and age. And yet, my friends, there are times in life when a man needs to pause and take stock."

As if speech and eyes journeyed along separate paths before converging at a single point, look and voice hardened. "I don't beat about the bush. To eat or to be eaten. That is the question. I have always defended this principle and I think I can say, with all modesty, that I shall be leaving my family rather more fortune than ill-fated destiny reserved for me in the cradle. But man cannot live by bread alone. He must also cultivate the spirit.

"Meaning culture."

As he spoke, the most implacable Benito Mallo's eyes slowly panned the assembled company, transforming the most ironic and amused expressions into attentive servility.

"Culture, gentlemen! And, within culture, the most sublime art of all. Poetry.

"With discretion and humility, I have recently given over some of my most intimate waking hours to her. I have sown the fields that lay fallow. I am well aware that there is a beast in every one of us, in some more than others. But the seasoned man is moved when he listens to the strings of his soul, as the child who winds up a music box in the attic."

The speaker took a swig of water and savoured it in his mouth, visibly pleased at pulling off in public this image of the beast and the child he had thought so long and hard about the night before. For their part, the audience of guests maintained a deathly silence, intimidated by Benito Mallo's blazing eyes, but no less intrigued to find out whether through his mouth it was sarcasm or disorder speaking.

"The reason for all these preambles is that I did not want

to take you completely by surprise. This has been a huge step for me, but I judged the occasion worthy of my daring. This is the result. I entrust these my poems to your leniency, aware that the novice's enthusiasm cannot remedy the lack of experience.

"To start with, a poem I composed in honour of our elders and ancestors."

Benito Mallo seemed to hesitate momentarily, as if touched by emotion, but soon recovered his natural elegant and undersized bearing, and began to declaim with a bard's verve.

> *The lives we lead are the rivers*
> *that flow out into the sea,*
> *which is the dying . . .*

"The joke was nearing its end," thought some of them. And they applauded Jorge Manrique's verses, laughing with a complicity that met with no response. On the contrary, Benito Mallo gave them a withering look and they shrank back in their seats until he reached the end of the poem.

"And now," he said, a Neronian menace to his voice, "now a composition that took a lot of work. A whole afternoon, at least, for as you see the first quatrain resists like an uncut diamond."

> *Violante has asked a sonnet of me,*
> *I never have been in such a dilemma . . .*

There was no laughter left. Not even for Lope de Vega. Only the odd murmur, which he dissolved with an icy stare. At the end, they applauded him, not any old how, but in the regimental manner of formal concerts.

"And finally, a poem I dedicate to youth. In particular to my granddaughter, Marisa, who is, after all, the reason we are here today. What would we not give to be young again? There are times when we chide them for being rebellious, but this is only natural at their age, the romantic spirit. Thinking of you, the young ones, I imagined a character who embodied freedom and came up with this pirate song."

> *Ten cannons on either side*
> *with a tail wind at full speed*
> *a brigantine does not cleave*
> *the waves of the sea but flies . . .*

There was an ovation with *vivas* for Don Benito, poet. He no longer cared if the tone was burlesque. He toasted the future. He downed a glass of brandy in one. He said, "And now enjoy yourselves!" And he disappeared, a solitary figure, into the house not to be seen for the whole of the rest of the day.

In the evening, Marisa, still embarrassed, asked for an explanation, but realized that he had gone into a daze. He had got drunk on his own. The bottle of herb liqueur stood empty on the table, a hint of golden viscosity in the glass and his voice.

"You see, girl? Power!"

When the Republic was created, he turned Republican. This only lasted a few months. Soon, his hero became the smuggler, banker and conspirator Juan March, known at the time as "The Last Pirate in the Mediterranean". With a glint in his eye, he told the story of what seemed to him one of the most brilliant expressions of wit in modern times. Like him, Don Juan read and wrote badly, but was a prodigy at doing sums. Primo de Rivera was amazed by this ability. At a meeting with his ministers, he addressed March and said, "So, Don Juan, what's seven times seven times seven times seven plus seven?" March replied in an instant, without time to think, "Two thousand four hundred and eight, my general." The dictator turned to the Finance Minister and said, "Listen and learn, distinguished minister!"

In 1933, Benito Mallo had sent seafood to Juan March in jail, which he would later escape from in the company of the prison governor. They had the same motto on their coat of arms: "Diners o dinars." Money or food. They believed that everything could be bought using these weapons.

The dogs bit now at her wrists, with savage affection, as if reproaching her. Marisa greeted the Portuguese gardener with magical delight.

"Hey, Alírio! How are you?"

Wrapped in the mist of burnt leaves, the gardener raised his arm in a slow, vegetal gesture. He returned to feeding the wood's censer, lost in a world of his own. She knew the rumours, Fronteira's secret radio waves. Which said that Alírio was the son of her grandfather's old employer, from the time he had set off as a young man to earn a living, and that Benito Mallo had not stopped until he had placed one of the employer's descendants in his service, less out of gratitude than in a twisted revenge on history. According to Fronteira's unwritten laws, there was no worse stigma than having served someone on the other side of the river. Be that as it may, in that walled universe, Alírio seemed the freest spirit. He lived apart from the others and moved about the estate like the silhouette of a sundial. As a girl, Marisa thought that the seasons were in part the creation of this gardener, who was so quiet he seemed dumb. He extinguished and kindled colours, as if he had an invisible underground fuse in the garden, connecting bulbs, trees and plants. The yellow never went out. The decree of winter turned off the last lights of the Chinese golden rose, but it was then, in that funereal atmosphere, that the lemons ripened and the souls came out with thousands of candles amid the canopy of mimosas. And, at the same time as the sparks flew on the brave mountain gorse and broom, the branches of forsythia caught fire. And by then the lanterns of the first irises and daffodils were appearing on the ground. Until in spring the splendour of gold dust exploded. It was Alírio who looked after the display with his lighter.

When Benito Mallo showed his distinguished visitors the manor's magnificent botany, among which the varieties of camellias stood out like a coat of arms, Alírio would follow them at a short distance, with his hands interlocked behind his back, like the master of keys of that cathedral. He would supply his lordship with the names of the different species when asked and with great tact make the necessary corrections.

"Alírio, how old do you think this bougainvillea is?"

"This wisteria, my lord, must be as old as the house."

Marisa would be amazed by the sentimental diagnosis with which he summed up the state of the trees, something he did only on unforeseen occasions, as if writing out a prescription in the air. "Those pale leaves! The lemon tree has melancholy. The rhododendron is genial. The chestnut has irregular breathing." The chestnut tree was like a secret home to Marisa. In the hundred-year-old trunk with its porthole, there was the space of a cabin from which you could spy on the world without being seen. The chestnut and she shared at least one secret, that of the chauffeur and Aunt Engracia. Ssssh.

When she told Da Barca what Alírio had said about the chestnut, the doctor had been astonished. "That gardener is a professor! A sage!" And then her lover said thoughtfully, "The trees are his windows. He's talking about himself."

Alírio fades now into the fog of fallen leaves.

Her grandfather appears at the top of the steps to receive her. His arms hang stiffly from his drooping shoulders and the cuffs of his jacket almost conceal his hands. All that is visible are the claws clenching his walking stick, its metal handle in the shape of a mastiff's head. The hawk in his eyes, Benito Mallo's unmistakable characteristic, is still alive, but there is about him the kind of resentment with which a lucid mind fights sclerosis. And that is why he comes down the steps.

"Do you need some help?"

"I'm not an invalid."

He tells her they can talk walking towards the rose garden, the sunny spell will not last, the winter sun is effective against what he calls this accursed rheumatism.

"You look very pretty," he said. "As ever."

Marisa recalled the last time they had seen each other. Her bleeding to death, her veins open in the bathtub. They had been forced to break down the door. He had wiped the scene from his mind.

"I've come to ask you a favour."

"You're in luck. That's my speciality."

"The war ended a year and eight months ago. As I understand it, there'll be pardons around Christmas."

Benito Mallo stopped and breathed in. The winter sun blinked on the majestic stained-glass window of the monkey-puzzle. "Irregular breathing," Marisa thought, searching with her eyes for the gardener's cloud of smoke.

"I'll be honest, Marisa. I did everything I could to have him killed. Now the greatest favour I can do you both is to do nothing."

"You can do more than you say."

He turned towards her and held her gaze, but not defiantly, with the curiosity of someone discovering a foreign face reflected in the river. If you stir the water, the face slips through your fingers, evasive, and re-forms like a second reality.

"Are you sure about that? You were too much for me."

She was going to tell him, "When will you realize there is such a thing as love?" And remind him, just to tease him, of the delirium he had suffered with the poetry. The episode of his sole recital had remained as an indelible farce in the annals of Fronteira. Benito Mallo had given the books from that enchanting shelf to a gypsy on his way to Coimbra and had them replaced with the volumes of Civil Law. But Marisa kept quiet. "Love, grandfather, does exist," was all she said.

"Love," he murmured, as if he had grains of salt in his mouth. And then he said in a hoarse, guttural voice, "I shall do no more. Follow your path. That is my favour."

Marisa did not protest. This was what she expected to achieve. According to Fronteira's laws, you have to throw in ten to get one out. Besides, her grandfather's word bound the whole clan, starting with her parents, submissive as lambs before Benito Mallo's whim. A family safe-conduct. No more manoeuvres, no more suitors for Penelope. Follow your path: I shall marry my imprisoned love.

"I'm going to marry him," she said.

Benito Mallo was silent. He gave the monkey-puzzle's vegetal window one last look and turned in the direction of the house. The walk was at an end.

The dogs were heard whining. Couto, the chauffeur who acted from time to time as his guardian, approached discreetly.

"Excuse me, my lord. The wife of that man from Rosal is here. The fugitive has reached Lisbon. And she wishes to thank you."

"Thank me? Tell her to pay what she owes and leave."

Marisa knew what they were referring to. Her grandfather was one of the victors. The repression in Fronteira had been especially cruel. An ossuary of skulls with bullet holes. Too much for the practically minded. And he was practically minded.

"The day after tomorrow," he said, turning back to Marisa, "a train will be leaving from Coruña. A special train. And your doctor will be on it."

16

THE CLOCK AT CORUÑA RAILWAY STATION HAD ALWAYS stopped at five minutes to ten. The boy selling newspapers sometimes had the impression that the minute hand, the longer of the two, trembled slightly before giving up again, unable to cope with its weight, like the wing of a hen. The boy thought that, deep down, the clock was right and that eternal malfunction was a stand in favour of realism. He would also like to have stopped, not at five minutes to ten, but four hours earlier, at the exact time his father was waking him in the hovel that was their home in Eirís. In winter and summer alike, a cloud of mist would settle there, compact damp that seemed gradually to be shrinking the house year after year, weighing down the roof, opening cracks in the walls. The boy was sure that, at night, one of its tentacles came down the chimney and stuck to the ceiling with its huge suckers, leaving behind those circular stains like the images of craters from a grey planet. The first waking landscape. The boy had to cross the city to Porta Real, where he would pick up the copies of *La Voz de Galicia*. Sometimes, in winter, he would run to chase away the cold from his feet. His father had made him some soles with pieces of car tyre. When he ran, the boy went vroom vroom vrooooom to clear a way through the mist.

Everyone knew the Madrid Express would be very late. The boy could not quite understand why they said late if the train was always on time two hours afterwards. But there they all were, taxi drivers, porters, old Betún, saying, "It looks as if it'll be late." They were the ones, set in their error, who were out of time. Were they to accept reality, he could sleep a little longer and would not have to slice through the mist with his imaginary horn.

Old Betún said to him,

"Yes, right. But, what if one day it arrives on time? You think you're pretty clever, eh, big-head?"

He would have liked to sell tobacco. But that was already the job of old Betún, who had been a bootblack previously. He sold tobacco and all sorts of things. His overcoat was a department store with an unexpected range of goods. For this reason he wore it in summer as well. But the boy sold newspapers only. Today could be a good day if some of those men were to buy them. Between them and the passengers on the Express, he could get rid of the lot and he would not have to go around calling out. He could wander home with his hands in his pockets and buy a small bottle of lemonade.

But none of those men marching in a line was going to buy the paper. Only one, tall, in an old suit without a tie and carrying a small leather case with polished corners, paused to look at the front page. A headline in large characters, "Hitler and Franco meet." The man in the suit without a tie and carrying the leather case continued reading as he moved away. The introduction to the piece was in bold, "The Führer met today with the Head of the Spanish State, General Franco, on the border between Spain and France. The meeting took place in the spirit of camaraderie that exists between the two nations." Given that he seemed to be interested in the article, were the man to buy the paper, he would find a commentary inside from the official news agency, Efe, stating that "the unique and sovereign figure of General Franco, in his already historic meeting with the Führer, has confirmed before Europe and the world the imperial will of our Homeland". But the man could not open the paper for the simple reason that he formed part of the line, even though he was almost the last one, and had a guard right behind him in a tricorne and cape, armed with a rifle, who did not halt before the young lad selling newspapers, but continued marking time.

No departure was due at that time, but this morning there was a train stationed at one of the main platforms. The carriages were built of wood, of the kind used for the transport of freight and cattle. The men lined up on the platform and placed the tiny clothes bundles they held in their hands on the ground. A guard counted them, calling out their numbers one by one. The boy thought that, if he were to be called by a number, he would like to be number 10, the one Chacho, his favourite footballer, wore on his shirt, who used to say,

"You've got to pass the ball as if it were hanging by a thread!" But a different guard came back and counted them again. A station clerk went along also, chanting out their numbers, much more quickly, as if competing with the others. "Maybe they're missing someone," the boy thought, and looked around and under the carriages. But who should he find except old Betún, who said to him?

"They're prisoners, big-head. Sick prisoners. With tuberculosis."

And he spat a large gobbet on to the ground and then trod on it as you would deliberately step on a bug.

From where he was, in line with the main entrance, and the ticket hall in between, the boy selling newspapers could keep a check on who came into the station. No surprise, therefore, that he should see the two women as soon as they alighted from the taxi. One was older, without being old, the other was younger, but they dressed in a similar way, as if they shared the same clothes and lipstick. "Right," thought the boy selling newspapers, "these two are almost certain to buy the paper." Because he could guess who was going to buy the paper or not as soon as he saw them, though, obviously, he got it wrong at times and was even taken by surprise. Once, for example, a blind man bought the paper. Aside from the passengers, he had some very special established customers, his regulars: the barefoot florist, the fishwife and the chestnut seller. No doubt, many journalists do not realize how useful newspapers can be. The chestnut seller, for example, would make cones as perfect as the arum lilies sold by the florist with bare feet.

"These two pale-faced, young ladies," thought the newspaper boy now, "are bound to buy a paper off me." But he got it wrong. And maybe he was to blame, because the younger one, initially, heeded his call and even drew up before the front page with the historic photograph of the Führer and Franco. But then she looked over towards the platform and it occurred to him to say,

"They're prisoners, madam. Sick prisoners. With tuberculosis."

And he was unsure whether to spit on the ground as old Betún had done, but he did not through lack of confidence and because the woman looked at him suddenly with tears in her eyes, as if she had grit in them, and started running towards the platform as if she were on a spring. Her medium-heeled shoes echoed around the whole station and even seemed to shake the minute hand out of its sleep.

The newspaper boy saw how the young woman anxiously went down the line of prisoners, without counting numbers, and finally embraced the man in the old suit without a tie. Now everything in the station came to a halt, even more so than usual, since after the commotion you get with arrivals or departures, the station would take on the atmosphere of a blind alley. Time stood still, except for the two of them embracing. Until a lieutenant who was there emerged from his own statue, walked towards them, and separated them as the pruner does with the stems of plants.

In the end, a guard passed by counting very slowly, as if he did not mind their thinking he could not count and, as he did so, he pointed at the prisoners with a baton in the form of a thick, red pencil.

"Like the one grandpa uses," thought the boy selling newspapers. "A carpenter's pencil."

17

"THEY EMBRACED IN THE STATION," HERBAL TOLD
Maria da Visitação. "None of us moved. We weren't quite
sure what to do. So the lieutenant went and separated them.
He pulled them apart, one from the other, as the pruner does
with the stems of plants.

"I had seen them like this once before, when no-one could
separate them.

"It was the day I found out they were in love. Prior to that
I'd never seen them together, nor could I have imagined that
Marisa Mallo and Daniel Da Barca would become a couple.
That was fine for a novel, but not for the reality of that time.
It was like sprinkling gunpowder on a censer.

"I actually came across them by chance, walking around
the Rosaleda in Santiago together at dusk, and I decided to
follow them. It was the end of autumn. They were engrossed
in conversation, not taking hold of one another, but drawing
closer when the gusts of wind raised swarms of dry leaves.
In the Alameda they had their photograph taken, one of those

that comes in a heart-shaped frame. The photographer had a bucket of water, in which he bathed the photographs. It started raining and everyone ran towards the bandstand, but I took shelter in the public lavatories. I imagined them laughing, their bodies touching, while the breeze dried the photograph. And when the sky cleared, night having fallen, I followed them again down the old city streets. The walk seemed as if it was never going to end, there was no getting close or caressing, and I began to get bored. Besides, it started raining again, that Santiago rain that works its way into your bronchial tubes and turns you into an amphibian. Even the stone horses have water coming out of their mouths."

"And what happened?" Maria da Visitação asked anxiously, uninterested in the horses with water coming out of their mouths.

"Oblivious of the rain, they stopped right in the middle of the Quintana dos Mortos. They must have been soaked, because I was dripping, and I'd been walking down the arcade. 'They're mad,' I thought, 'they'll catch their death of cold. Blasted doctor!' But then that happened. The Berenguela."

"Who's the Berenguela?"

"It's a bell. The Berenguela is a bell of the Cathedral, overlooking the Quintana. At the first stroke, they embraced. And it was as if they were never going to let go, because it was midnight. The Berenguela chimes so slowly it's supposed to be good for giving the wine in the barrels that extra something, but I don't know how it doesn't drive all the clocks mad."

"How did they embrace, Herbal?" the girl from the nightclub asked him.

"I've seen man and woman get up to all sorts, but these two, they drank each other. They licked the water off each other with their lips and tongues. They sucked in each other's ears, the bowl of their eyes, from the breast to the neck upwards. They were so drenched they must have felt naked. They kissed like two fish."

Suddenly, Herbal drew two parallel lines with the pencil on the white paper napkin. And then he drew thicker, shorter lines across. The sleepers.

The train, the train lost in the snow.

Maria da Visitação noticed the white of Herbal's eyes. A white gone slightly yellow, like smoked lard. Against that background, the iris flared up in the silences like a piece of burning wood. Allowed to grow, the white of his hair might have acquired a venerable tone, but it had the appearance of darkened grey due to a conscript's drastic haircut. He was already advanced in years, you could even say old. But he had a lean, tense constitution, like reddened, knotty wood. Maria da Visitação had begun to think about age, having turned twenty in October. She knew older people who seemed a lot younger than they were due to a kind of happy-go-lucky pact with time. Other people, and Manila, who owned the bar, was one of them, had an almost pathetic relationship with age, trying to cover up its traces in a vain obsession, the adornments, the overly tight dresses and wealth of jewellery, doing nothing except to accentuate the contrast. But she only knew one person, and that was Herbal, who stayed younger through misfortune. It was unclear whether his breathlessness was because he wanted or did not want to breathe. The rage against the slow passing of time came to the surface whenever things got difficult at night. It was enough for him to look daggers from the end of the bar, for a client holding the stage to cough up the money without a murmur.

"Sometimes, when I wake up out of breath, I have the sensation we're still there, stuck on a snow-covered track in the province of Leon. And there's a wolf watching us, watching the train, so I lower the half window and aim with the rifle on the glass and the painter says to me, 'What are you doing?' 'Can't you see?' I reply, 'I'm going to kill that wolf.' 'Don't spoil the painting,' he says. 'It took me a lot of hard work.'

"The wolf turns around and leaves us on our own, on a siding."

"Another one, sir," a guard tells the lieutenant. "In coach nine."

The lieutenant swears the way you do in the face of an invisible enemy. When it came to the dead, he did not like the number three. One corpse is a corpse. The second keeps the first company. He had remained impassive. But from there on up was a stack of corpses. A situation. He was still a young man. He cursed that mission without the slightest glory. To command a forgotten train, laden with defeat and tuberculosis, and on top of that blocked by nature's absurd, mad shells. An unstitched war rag. He put a startling hypothesis out of his head: I cannot arrive in Madrid at the head of a funeral parlour.

"Three dead already. What the hell is going on?"

"They drown in their blood, sir. They get a coughing fit and they drown in their own blood."

Withering look: "Yes, I know what happens. I don't need it explained. And what about the doctor? What's the doctor doing?"

"He hasn't stopped, sir. From one coach to the next. He said to tell you we should empty out the last carriage and set it aside for the corpses."

"Well, then do it. I'll go with this chap here," he said, referring to Herbal, "to that damned station. Meanwhile inform the driver. We shall move this train even if it's on our hands and knees."

The lieutenant looked anxiously outside. On one side, the plain, white as nothing. On the other, a frozen archaeology of stranded trains and sheds that resembled pantheons of railway skeletons.

"This is worse than war!"

Inmates had been brought together on that train from the prisons in the north of Galicia, suffering from an advanced stage of TB. In the misery following the war, tuberculosis spread like a plague, a situation made worse by the humidity of the Atlantic coast. Their final destination was a prison hospital in the Valencia mountain range. But first they had to reach Madrid. A passenger train at that time could take eighteen hours to cover the distance between Coruña and North Station in the capital.

"Ours was termed a Special Transport Train," Herbal said to Maria da Visitação. "Special is exactly what it was!"

When the inmates boarded the carriages, many of them had already eaten their allowance of food: a tin of sardines. To keep them warm they had each been given a blanket. The snow put in its appearance in the heights around Betanzos and did not leave them until Madrid. The Special Transport Train took its seven hours to reach Monforte, the railway junction connecting Galicia and the Meseta. But the worst was yet to come. They still had to cross the mountains of Zamora and Leon. When the train stopped in Monforte, darkness was already falling. The prisoners shivered with cold and fever at the same time.

"I was frozen as well," Herbal continued. "Those of us on guard detail travelled in a passenger carriage, with seats and windows, behind the locomotive. It was a steam engine, which had difficulty pulling the train, as if it too suffered from tuberculosis.

"Yes, I had volunteered. I put myself forward as soon as I heard about that train taking TB sufferers to a prison hospital in Valencia. I was convinced I had the very same disease, but covered it up the whole time, avoided the medical examinations, which for me was not difficult. I thought they'd lay me off sick, with a miserable wage, and I'd be sidelined for good. I didn't want to go back to my parents' village or to my sister's house. The last time I had spoken to my father was coming back from Asturias. We argued a lot. I refused to work, told him I was on leave and said that he was an animal. And then my father, with a calmness I didn't know he possessed, replied, 'I didn't kill anyone. When we were kids and got called up for Morocco, we took to the hills. Yes, I am an animal, but I didn't kill anyone. Sit back and feel satisfied if, as an old man, you can say the same!' I haven't spoken to my father since.

"When I heard about the train, I went back to see Sergeant Landesa, who by then had been promoted. 'Arrange for me to go with them, sir, in the hospital guard. I need the change of climate. And that doctor, Doctor Da Barca, is going too, you recall. I believe he is still in contact with the resistance. I shall, of course, keep you informed.'"

The lieutenant, Herbal and the driver approach the Leonese station. The snow covers their boots. They shake it off on the platform. The lieutenant is fuming. He is planning to shout at the stationmaster, tell him a few things. But out of the office comes a commanding officer. The lieutenant is caught off guard and takes a while to stand to attention. The commanding officer, before he speaks, eyes him severely and awaits the gesture of compliance with rank. The lieutenant clicks his heels, stands to attention and salutes with mechanical precision. "At your orders, my commander." It is very cold, but he has sweat on his forehead. "I am in charge of the Special Train and . . . "

"The Special Train? What train are you talking about, lieutenant?"

The lieutenant's voice trembles. He does not know where to begin.

"The train, the train of prisoners with TB, sir. We've three dead already."

"The train of prisoners with TB? Three dead? What are you telling me, lieutenant?"

The driver is about to speak, "I can explain, sir." But the commanding officer, with an energetic gesture, shuts him up.

"We left Coruña, sir, forty-eight hours ago. What we have here is a Special Transport Train. With prisoners, sick prisoners. With tuberculosis. We should have been in Madrid by now. But there seems to have been some confusion. In Leon we were allowed through, but on a diversion towards the north. This went on for several hours. When we realized, we turned back. But it was not easy, commander. Since then, we have been sitting on a siding. We were told there were other special trains."

"Indeed there are, lieutenant. You ought to know," said the commanding officer sardonically. "The north-west coast is being reinforced. Or have you not heard of the Second World War?"

He called the signalman.

"What can you tell me about a train of prisoners with TB?"

"A train of prisoners with TB? That went through yesterday, sir."

"There was some confusion," the lieutenant was about to explain once more. But he realized that the commanding officer was gazing in astonishment at the railway lines.

Swaying, walking sluggishly and swept along by the snow, a small procession drew near with a man on a stretcher. Before his mind could confirm the vision to him, he sensed what was happening. At the head walked that damnable doctor, flanked by two of the guards. As they came closer, Lieutenant Goyanes spliced that slow sequence with other recent images. The unrestrained embrace in the station, which he cut using the pliers of his hands, disturbed by that unending kiss that upset the foundations of reality like an earthquake. The conversation that followed on the train, an aborted approach on his part. He had tried to justify himself with a splash of humour, without it sounding like an apology,

"Someone had to separate you. Quite clearly you'd have kept us waiting till the cows came home. Ha, ha! Was that your wife then? You're a lucky man."

He realized that everything he was saying had a wounding double meaning. Doctor Da Barca made no reply, as if all he could hear were the din of the train taking him further away from the warm, perfumed embrace of woman. The lieutenant had told him to take a seat in his carriage. After all, he was also in charge of the expedition. They had things to talk about.

Leaving behind the large tunnel that blotted out the urban horizon, the train entered the green and blue watercolour of the Burgo estuary. Doctor Da Barca blinked as if the beauty hurt his eyes. From their boats, with long rakes, the fishermen combed the bottom of the sea for shellfish. One of them stopped working and looked in the direction of the train, his hand shielding his face, erect on the sea's swaying surface.

Doctor Da Barca recalled his friend the painter. He used to like painting scenes of work in the fields and at sea, but not according to the traditional clichés, which turned them into pretty, bucolic pictures. On his friend the painter's canvases, people were shown merging into the earth and the sea. Their faces seemed furrowed by the very plough that clove the earth. The fishermen were captives of the very nets that seized the fish. It reached the point where their bodies fragmented. Sickle arms. Sea eyes. Face stones. Doctor Da Barca empathized with the fisherman standing erect on his boat, looking at the train. He may have wondered where it was going and what it was taking there. The distance and the din of the engine would prevent him from hearing the terrible litany of coughing ringing out in the squalor of the cattle trucks like skin tambourines soaked in blood. The panorama brought to mind a fable: with its cries, the cormorant flying over the fisherman was telegraphing the truth about the train. He remembered the bitterness his friend the painter felt when he stopped receiving the avant-garde art magazines he was sent from Germany: the worst illness that can strike is the suspension of conscience. Doctor Da Barca opened his case and pulled out a brief treatise with worn covers, *The Biological Roots of Aesthetic Feeling*, by Doctor Roberto Nóvoa Santos.

Lieutenant Goyanes sat down opposite. He looked at the small book's cover out of the corner of his eye. This Doctor Da Barca, he calculated, had to be a little older than he was, but not much. After the incident of their departure, when he was informed that he was the doctor, he had adopted an attitude of camaraderie, but with the superiority of a hiking guide. Now, unconcerned about interrupting the other's reading, he began to tell him how he had also gone to University, taking a few courses in Philosophy, before enlisting in Franco's army, where he had started out as second lieutenant. After that he had decided to continue with a military career. "Philosophy!" he exclaimed in an ironic tone. "I too was attracted by Marx and all those prophets of social redemption. Like il duce Mussolini. He was a socialist, you know? Yes, of course you know. Till the blessed day the Warrior Philosopher turned up. Destroyer of the Present. He freed me from the flock of slaves."

Doctor Da Barca carried on reading, deliberately ignoring him, but the other knew how to make him talk.

"That was when I stopped worrying about the apes and became interested in the gods."

He had hit the nail on the head. The doctor at last put down his book and stared at him,

"I'd never have guessed, lieutenant."

He burst out laughing and slapped him on the knees.

"Good, good," he said, standing up, "a Republican with balls. Stick to worrying about the apes."

There was no time for jokes after that. Things began to get complicated as if the train were driven by the devil. In Monforte the expected replenishment of food for the prisoners did not arrive. Then came that calvary in the mountains of snow. The doctor moving tirelessly from carriage to carriage.

The last time the lieutenant had seen him he had been on his knees, by the light of an oil lamp, cleaning the dark, clotted blood from the spikes of the beard of the first corpse.

Snowflakes covered the doctor's hair, which had curled. One of the guards stepped forward to give explanations, "He told us it was a matter of life or death, sir, and that you had authorized it." In front of the commander, in the station whipped by the blizzard, Lieutenant Goyanes felt obliged to offer a show of authority. He snatched the guard's rifle and with the butt knocked Da Barca down.

"He did not have my permission!"

On the ground, the doctor strokes the wound with the back of his hand. It is bleeding where the blow has landed, on his cheek. Unhurriedly, he takes a handful of snow and applies it like a balm. "An oil painting with blood and snow," says the painter inside Herbal's head. "The ointment of history. Why don't you help him to stand up?"

"You're mad," mutters the guard.

"Help him, can't you see the reason he's doing all this is to get us back on the blasted move?"

Corporal Herbal hesitates. Suddenly, he steps forward and lends the wounded man a hand so that he can get to his feet.

"He reacted with complete surprise," he told Maria da Visitação. "He may have been remembering the day he was arrested, when I knocked him about. But then he returned the lieutenant's blow with a piercing look. He had that about him. He made the other feel smaller."

Coughing. The signalman turned to the sick man on the

126

stretcher as if the bell on the crank telephone were ringing.

The commander moves the lieutenant to one side,

"Now what the hell is going on?"

"This man is not far off a final haemoptysis," Doctor Da Barca tells him. "Any moment now he'll drown in his own blood. We've lost three already."

"And what's the point of bringing him here? I know what tuberculosis is. If he's going to die, well, he'll have to die. The nearest hospital is miles away."

"There's only one thing to do. We mustn't lose any more time. I need a room with plenty of light, a table and boiled water."

The signalman's table had a pane of glass on the wood. The glass covered a map of the Spanish railways. They threw a blanket on top and laid the sick man down. In the small saucepan on the stove, the water with the syringe needle began to boil. The bubbling sound was similar to the patient's breathing. Witnessing the preparations for that crude operation, Herbal attempted to listen to his own chest. The sea's tickling on the spongy sand. He rolled a ball of spit against his palate to see if he could detect the sweet taste of blood. Only the painter was aware of his anguish, the secret of his hidden illness. He kept watch on the others' symptoms. He pretended not to care, but made a mental note whenever a medical comment referred to TB. He learnt from every sign of his body.

"The Ailing Generation! The best Galician artists died very young, of tuberculosis," the painter had told him. "The scythe in Galicia has an artistic streak, Herbal. If you've got it, yours is a famous disease. They were very attractive too, with a melancholy beauty. Women were crazy about them."

"Well, thank you. That's some consolation."

"Not about you, Herbal."

He looked at the sick man before him, lying on the signalman's table. He was only a boy, young and fresh-faced. But in the expression of his eyes there was an ancient lichen. He knew his story. His name was Seán. A deserter. He had spent three years on the run on Mount Pindo, living like a rock-animal. There were dozens of men in those caves. When they scoured the area, the Civil Guard could never find them. Until they broke the code of signals. The washerwomen were accomplices, writing messages over the thickets with the colours of their clothes.

"What are you going to do?" the commander asked him.

"A pneumothorax," Doctor Da Barca said, "an artificial pneumothorax. The idea is for air to enter the chest, compressing the lungs and stopping the haemorrhage."

And then he assembled the syringe, looked at Seán calmly and winked at him in encouragement.

"Let's to it, eh, my friend? It's only a prick in between the ribs."

Just so. Only a prick. A bee's sting in the wolf's chest.

But then the doctor is quiet, so absorbed he seems to X-ray the chest with his eyes. He slowly finds a place for the needle and punctures very quickly. Herbal helps to hold the patient down by the wrist. The boy clenches his fists, digs his nails into his own palm. The doctor stands still, the needle sticking into the boy's chest, attentive to the bag of air. On the signalman's table, in the caverns of man, the sound of running water, the organ of the wind.

"The train left the very same afternoon," Herbal told Maria da Visitação. "At all the stations it passed straight through. The train lost in the snow was now a phantom train. When it did stop, it was briefly, and no-one came near. A couple of us would alight in order to sort out the food supplies. We returned empty-handed. All the stations smelt of hunger," said Herbal, looking at the air freshener on the table. "And yet, in spite of everything, I remember one detail. In Medina del Campo a man banged on the window and greeted Da Barca. Then he disappeared. The train was already leaving when he returned with a sack of chestnuts. I caught it almost in midair, at the door to the carriage. He shouted, 'They're for the doctor!' He was a big bloke, with laboured breathing. Genghis Khan. Among the chestnuts, a wallet. 'He must have swiped it right here, in the station,' I thought. I was going to keep it. In the end, I took half the notes and handed the sack to the doctor."

"And what happened to that boy, the deserter?" Maria da Visitação asked anxiously.

"He died in Porta Coeli. Yes, he died in that hospital which was known as the Doorway to Heaven."

18

DOCTOR DA BARCA WAS WRITING A LOVE LETTER. That is why he kept crossing out. He thought that language was extremely poor for such a task, and he was sorry not to have a poet's lack of shame. He did have when it came to the other prisoners. Part of his therapy consisted in encouraging them to recall their loves and to put a few words in the post. He lent his hand good-humouredly to writing some of those letters. "Her name's Eileen, doctor." "Eileen?" "Eileen . . . " "*The scent of unripe lemons and tangerine.* What do you think?"

"She'll like it, doctor. She's very natural."

But when it came to him, he felt that, in effect, all love letters were ridiculous. At times he was amazed at the things a sick man could say without affectation. "Doctor, write down that she's not to worry. As long as she's alive, I shan't die ever. When I'm short of air, I breathe through her mouth."

And another, "Write down that I'll be back. I'll be back to seal all the leaks in the roof."

He crossed out the opening again. Today's had to be a

special letter. Finally, he wrote, "Wife." It was then he heard a knock at the door of his room. It was late for the prison hospital, after eleven o'clock at night. Perhaps it was an emergency. He opened the door, prepared to disguise his displeasure. Mother Izarne. On another occasion he would have joked about her Mercedarian order's white habit, "Ah, I thought you were an ectoplasmic crumb!" but this time he noticed an air of unreality that disturbed him in his modesty. The nun had a woman's saucy smile. Suddenly, with no other greeting, she produced a bottle of brandy from underneath her skirt.

"For you, doctor. For your wedding night!"

And she scuttled off down the corridor, like someone fleeing cheerful audacity, leaving behind an aura of blazing eyes.

Bluish-greyish-green. Eyes slightly torn, with a fold of skin in the shape of a half-moon on her eyelids.

Like Marisa's. "God did not exist," thought Da Barca, "but providence does."

It had been Mother Izarne in person who had come to him that evening in high spirits with the telegram confirming the celebration of the wedding ceremony. That same morning, Marisa had said "I do" in the church in Fronteira. He knew the time. In Porta Coeli, seven hundred miles away, the doctor was accompanying his patients on their morning walk. He wore a white shirt and his old festive suit. Between pines and olive trees, he closed his eyes and said, "I do, of course I do."

"Hey, everyone! The doctor's daydreaming."

"My friends, I have some news. I have just got married!"

131

"The others had an inkling," Herbal told Maria da Visitação, "because they surrounded him shouting, 'Congratulations, Da Barca!' They each had a handful of broom flowers in their pockets, which they had picked up along the way, and they showered him with that mountain gold. The two of them had got married by proxy. Do you know how that works? Her brother, Fernando, took the bridegroom's place in the church, and the doctor had to complete a document before a notary. In all of this he was helped a great deal by the Mother Superior, Mother Izarne, who even signed as a witness. She took as much interest as if she were the one getting married."

"I think you were jealous!" Maria da Visitação remarked, smiling.

"She was a very pretty nun," said Herbal. "And very clever. She did look a bit like Marisa. There was a kind of resemblance. But she was a nun, of course. She hated me. I don't know why she hated me so much. When it came to it, I was a guard and she was the Mother Superior of the nuns who worked in the prison hospital. We were, at least I thought we were, on the same side."

Herbal looked out of the open window, as if searching for the distant, flickering light of memory. It was dusk, the time the headlights of the cars began to appear on the Fronteira road.

"One day she caught me opening the prisoners' correspondence. I was interested most of all in the letters addressed to Doctor Da Barca, of course. I read them very closely."

"For your report?" Maria da Visitação asked him.

"If I spotted something strange, that's right. I had to fill out a report. My attention was drawn particularly to his correspondence with a friend, by the name of Souto, in which he only ever spoke about football. His idol was Chacho, a Deportivo da Coruña player. I found it strange, this passion for football in Doctor Da Barca, whom I'd never heard enthuse about the game. But in his letters – because I read them as well, the control went both ways – he would say things as pertinent as that you should pass the ball hanging by a thread, or that the ball should do the running and not the player, that is why it was round. I liked Chacho as well, so I let them go and didn't give them another thought. In reality, the ones that interested me most were Marisa's. I discussed them with the dead painter. He was particularly fond of one that had a love poem that spoke of blackbirds. I held it back for a week. I carried it in my pocket to re-read it. There was no-one who wrote to me . . .

"But what happened was that one day Mother Izarne came into the porters' lodge and caught me brimming with confidence, with a pile of opened envelopes scattered across the desk. I carried on as normal. I assumed she knew all about the control of correspondence. But she worked herself up into a fury. I said to her a bit nervously, 'It's OK, Mother, it's official procedure. And don't shout so much, absolutely everybody's going to hear you.' At which point she got even more enraged and said, 'Take your dirty hands off that letter!' She snatched it from me, with the unfortunate result that it tore in two.

"She looked at the opening. It was Marisa Mallo's letter to Doctor Da Barca, the one with the love poem that talked about blackbirds.

"The pieces trembled in her hands. But she carried on reading.

"I said to her,

"'It's of no interest, Mother. There's no mention of politics.'

"She said to me,

"'Pig.

"'Pig in a tricorne hat.'

"Since arriving, I had been feeling well. Compared to the climate in Galicia, Porta Coeli's was one long spring. But, during that unexpected altercation with the nun, I again felt the damned bubbling in my chest, the sense of breathlessness arriving.

"She must have noticed the terror coming into my eyes. Every one of those nuns was worth a mutual insurance company. She said,

"'You are ill.'

"'Heavens above, Mother, don't say that. It's nerves, that's all. Nerves getting inside my head.'

"'That is an ailment as well,' she said. 'It is cured by prayer.'

"'I already pray. But it doesn't get any better.'

"'Then go to hell!'

"She was very clever. And had a fearful temper. She left with the letter torn in two.

"I discussed what had happened with a police inspector, by the name of Arias, who used to come up from time to time from Valencia, without referring, needless to say, to the matter of my health. 'Never get between a nun and where she wants to go,' he exclaimed laughing, 'or you can be certain you'll end up in hell.'

"Inspector Arias, with his trimmed moustache, was a great theoretician. He said,

"'Spain will never have a perfect dictatorship that runs like clockwork, to match Hitler's. And do you know why, corporal? Because of women. Half the women in Spain are whores and the other half are nuns. I am sorry for you. I got the first half.

"'Ha, ha, ha!'

"An old barracks joke.

"'I can tell the odd story, but I'm terrible at jokes,' I said to him.

"'There once was a dog named Joke. The dog died and that was the end of the Joke.'

"'Ha, ha, ha! That's ridiculous, my Galician friend!'"

Hell. Never get between a nun and where she wants to go. Herbal took the opportunity to tell the inspector it would be better for him to stop dealing with the correspondence.

"Absolutely," the other said. "We'll have it sent via the police station."

"Do you think she liked him?" Maria da Visitação asked, getting to the point that interested her.

"He had a certain something, as I told you. To women he was like a pied piper."

No-one was quite sure when Doctor Da Barca slept. His vigils were always with a book in his hand. There were times he would collapse from exhaustion in the patients' block or on the ground outside, the open book keeping his chest warm. She began to lend him works that they would then discuss. Their conversations continued in the fine weather, into the night, when the patients went outside for a breath of fresh air.

Under the moon, they would walk up and down the path that led to the mount of pines.

What Herbal did not know was that the nun Izarne had also on one occasion told Doctor Da Barca to go to hell. It was in the spring after his arrival in Porta Coeli and on account of Saint Teresa.

She said,

"You disappoint me, doctor. I knew you were not religious, but I thought you were a sensitive man."

He said,

"Sensitive? In the Book of Life Saint Teresa writes, 'My heart hurt.' And this was true, her heart, the viscus, did hurt. She had angina and later suffered a heart attack. Doctor Nóvoa Santos, the master pathologist, went to Alba, where the reliquary is kept, and examined the saint's heart. He was an honest man, believe me. Now, he reaches the conclusion that what is understood to be a wound, inflicted by the angel's dart, is nothing other than the atrioventricular groove, the fissure separating the right atrium from the ventricle. But he also finds a scar, of the type left behind by sclerosis, indicating a heart attack. The clinical eye, as the master Nóvoa underlines, cannot explain a poem, but a poem is quite capable of revealing to the clinical eye what it does not know. And that poem, *I live but outside myself, I await a life so high, that not dying yet I die.* Not dying yet I die! That poem . . . "

"Is a marvel!"

"Yes. It is also a marvellous diagnosis."

"That is very crude of you, doctor. We are talking here of poetry, of some sublime verses, and all you can do is talk to me of viscera like a forensic scientist."

"Forgive me, but I am a pathologist."

"Indeed, more like a bar-tologist!"

"Listen, Izarne. Mother Izarne. These verses are exceptional. No pathologist could describe an ailment in the same way. She transforms that weakness, the transitory death causing her the angina, into an expression of culture or, if you prefer, of the spirit. A sigh become a poem."

"To you, not dying yet I die is a sigh, and that's it?"

"Yes. A sigh, albeit a highly-qualified one."

"Mother of God! You are so cold, so cynical, so . . . "

"So what?"

"So proud. You do not recognize God out of pure pride."

"Quite the opposite. Out of pure modesty. If Saint Teresa and the mystics really are addressing themselves to God, it is with an arrogance such as falls within the boundaries of pathology. *To see God who is my prisoner!* To be honest, I prefer the God of the Old Testament. High in the highest, directing the stars, like someone directing a Hollywood film. I prefer to think that the God of Saint Teresa has a real incarnation, an absent-minded human being who was not even informed of the saint's yearning. *How bitter is the life in which the Lord cannot be enjoyed!* Why not conclude that she was taken with an impossible love? Besides, she was the granddaughter and daughter of Jewish converts. She was forced to use more guile. Hence she talks of prison and the soul's irons. She expresses the angina, her physical weakness, but also a real, impossible love. Some of her confessors were intelligent, very attractive men . . . "

"I'm leaving. I find what you're saying repugnant."

"But why? I believe in the soul, Mother Izarne."

"You believe in the soul? Well, you talk about it as if it were a secretion . . . "

"Not exactly. We might go so far as to say that the soul's material substratum are the cellular enzymes."

"You are a monster, a monster who thinks he's funny."

"Saint Teresa compares the soul to a medieval castle, *the whole is a single diamond cut by the divine glazier.* Why a diamond? If I were a poet, and I wish I were, I would speak of a snowflake. No two are the same. They melt away in existence, in the sun's rays, as if to say, 'Immortality, how boring!' Body and soul are bound together. As music to an instrument. The injustice that gives rise to social suffering is basically the most terrible soul-destroying machine."

"And why do you think I'm here? I am not a mystic. I fight against suffering, the suffering that you, the heroes of one and the other side, cause in ordinary people."

"You're wrong again. There'll be no trace of me left. You

won't find me in any calendar of saints' days. In the words of the Nazi doctors, I belong to the field of ballast lives, lives that don't deserve to be lived. I shan't even have the relief of seeing myself seated, like you, at the right hand of God. But I shall tell you something, Mother Izarne. If God exists, he is a schizoid being, a kind of Doctor Jekyll and Mr Hyde. And you belong to his good side."

"Why do you make me tear my hair out?"

"I don't even know what colour it is."

Mother Izarne took off her white wimple and shook her head, freeing her long, russet hair.

She said,

"Now you know. And go to hell!"

And he said,

"I shouldn't mind finding there a star."

"Do you think there are beings on other planets?" Herbal asked Maria da Visitação suddenly.

"I don't know," she said with an ironic smile. "I'm not from here. I don't have any papers."

"The nun and Doctor Da Barca," Herbal continued, "were always talking about the sky. Not heaven, but the starry sky. After dinner, when the patients lazed about outside, the two of them would compete at identifying the stars. Apparently a sage had been burnt many years ago for saying there was life on other planets. In those days there was no beating about the bush. They both thought that there was, that there were people up above. They agreed about that. And they thought it would be a wonderful thing for the world. I'm not so sure.

There'd be more people wanting a piece of their own land. Considering how well-read they were, they were a bit crazy. But I found them amusing to listen to. The truth is if you sit and look at the sky for any length of time it fills with more and more stars. There are even some we see that no longer exist. The light takes so long to get here that, by the time it reaches us, the star's gone out. Amazing, isn't it? To be seeing what no longer exists.

"Maybe it's all like that."

"But what happened next?" Maria da Visitação asked impatiently.

"They caught him and that was the end of the hospital. This really messed things up. The climate suited me, and it wasn't a bad life. I was a guard who didn't guard. No-one was going to escape. What for? The whole of Spain was a prison. That was the truth. Hitler had invaded Europe and was winning all the battles. The Republicans had nowhere to go. Who was going to move in a situation like that? The odd couple of madmen. Including Doctor Da Barca.

"We had been in the hospital for little over a year. One day Inspector Arias turned up with some other policemen. They looked very serious. They said to me, 'Bring us that doctor by the ears.' I knew, of course, who they were talking about. I pretended not to, 'What doctor?' 'Come off it, corporal, bring us that Daniel Da Barca fellow.'"

The doctor had just done the rounds of the patients in the main building. He was going over new developments with the nuns who were nurses, Mother Izarne being one of them.

"Doctor Da Barca, you'll have to accompany me. They wish to see you."

The white cortège exchanged silent glances.

"Who wishes to see me?" he said with ironic suspicion. "Have they come with the coal?"

"'No,' I said. 'They've brought sticks.'

"It was the first time that a joke had come to me spontaneously. The doctor seemed to appreciate it. On his part, it was the first time he had turned to me without giving the impression he was wasting his energy. Mother Izarne, on the other hand, looked at me in horror."

"Hello there, Chacho," said Inspector Arias when the doctor was before him. "How's that left foot of yours?"

The doctor put on a brave face. He replied in the same sardonic manner, "I've been injured this season."

The inspector dropped his cigarette, which he had not finished smoking, and crushed it slowly into the ground as if it were a lizard's loose tail.

"We'll see about that at the police station. We've some good orthopaedists there."

He took Doctor Da Barca by the arm. There was no need to push him. He allowed himself to be led towards the car.

"I think someone should explain to me what is going on," said Mother Izarne, confronting the inspector.

"He's a ringleader, Mother. He conducts the orchestra."

"This man is mine!" she exclaimed, her eyes ablaze. "He belongs to the hospital. He has been admitted here!"

"You look after your kingdom, Mother," Inspector Arias

rejoined coldly, without stopping, "and leave hell to us."

One of the other policemen was still heard to mutter the remark,

"I'll be damned! That nun's got character."

"More than the Pope," the inspector said in an angry voice. "Now for fuck's sake get us out of here."

"I had never seen a nun cry before," Herbal told Maria da Visitação. "It's a very strange sensation. Like a walnut statue that weeps."

"It's OK, Mother! Doctor Da Barca always lands on his feet."

"The truth is I wasn't exactly an expert at consoling people. She told me to go to hell for a second time."

They brought him back after three days, long enough for him to have lost weight. One of the guards who escorted him told Herbal that the police had been searching for this Chacho fellow for some time. It had never occurred to them that he might be singing from inside the cage. He was a legend in the resistance. The player combinations he suggested in his letters, the comments regarding footballing tactics, were in fact coded messages for the underground organization. From his time as a Republican leader and his stay in prison, Da Barca was a walking archive. He stored all the information in his head. His texts, giving evidence of the repression, were being published in the English and American press. He was going to be put back on trial.

"But he's already got a life sentence!"

"Then they'll give him another one. In case he resurrects."

"I suppose he had been badly beaten," Herbal said to Maria

da Visitação, "but the doctor made no reference to the time he had spent in the police station, not even when Mother Izarne came to him and searched his face for marks of torture. He had a bruise on his neck, under his ear. The nun massaged it with the tips of her fingers, but soon withdrew her hand as if she had received a shock."

"Thank you for your interest, Mother. They are sending me to another, damper hotel than this. To Galicia. To San Simón Island."

She looked away towards a window. The boundary stood out between the field and the hillside, against the golden background of broom. But then she reacted with a novice's smile.

"You see? God closes one door and opens another. Now you'll be close to her."

"Yes. That is a good thing."

"As soon as you can, give her a big hug from me. Don't forget that I had a hand in your marriage."

"I'll do that. I shan't forget."

19

DANIEL DA BARCA QUICKLY SCANNED THE ROWS of windows looking for the reflection of a wimple shaped like a dove. But he found none. He had said goodbye to all the prisoners, his patients, and a cluster of Mercedarian nuns had gathered at the exit. She was not among them. "Mother Izarne is at prayer in chapel," the eldest nun told him, as if she were on an errand. He nodded. They watched him expectantly. The breeze swayed their habits in a white farewell. "I should say a few words," he thought. "Or better nothing." He smiled at them.

"My blessing, Mothers!" And he made the sign of the cross in the air like a dean.

They laughed like young girls.

"And what did you say?" Maria da Visitação asked Herbal.

"I didn't say anything. What was I going to say! I left as I had arrived. As his shadow."

The scene must have affected Sergeant García in some way. "They're orders, doctor," he said as he handcuffed him, seemingly upset at having to interrupt their leave-taking with chains. In the warrant informing him of the custody of the prisoner, which he would carry out in the company of Corporal Herbal, who was heading back to his posting in Galicia, he was told that he would be dealing with a "prominent element opposed to the regime", sentenced to life imprisonment. He had, therefore, made the journey up to the prison hospital in an alert frame of mind, ill at ease with a transfer mission that would cause him to travel the breadth of Spain, on trains that crawled along like penitents with the cross on their shoulders. He had been relieved to see the prisoner with that cluster of captive nuns. He had once heard an old warrant officer say that an intellectual is like a gypsy: once he has fallen, he never revolts. The one that was a corpse, he thought as they settled on to the first train, from Valencia to Madrid, was the colleague he had been given as an escort. Boredom itself. Like a drunk who has sobered up in the morning. Like a punctual gravedigger. By the time they arrived in Vigo, a cobweb would have formed on his eyelashes.

"Forgive me for interrupting your reading, doctor, but I should like a consultation. It's something I've been toying with for some time. You are a doctor, you ought to know about this. Why are men always up for it? You know what I mean."

"Are you talking about sex?"

"That's right," said the sergeant, laughing. He rubbed, rub-a-dub, his hands up and down, "I'm talking about 'it'. Animals stop, don't they? I mean. They're on heat and then they stop. But humans don't. The flagpole ever rigid!"

"Is that what happens to you?"

"I see a woman and my mind goes into overdrive. It happens to the lot of us, doesn't it? You're not going to tell me it's a disease?"

"No, not exactly. It's a symptom. This tends to happen in countries where it's not done a great deal." He mimicked the sergeant's gesture of rubbing, rub-a-dub, his hands, "You know what I mean."

Sergeant García found the remark amusing. He roared with laughter and looked over towards Herbal. "He's a subtle one, eh, corporal?"

"I didn't feel very well," Herbal told Maria da Visitação. Over a year had gone by since the outward journey. They had changed trains in Madrid, and in North Station they had caught an express for Galicia. They were going to go back the route of the train lost in the snow. It was spring, and the doctor's handcuffs glinted in the sunlight like wristwatches. But Herbal did not feel very well. He sensed his own paleness as if he had lain down on a cold, damp pillow.

"Are you all right, corporal?"

"Yes, sergeant. The train makes me sleepy."

"That will be low blood pressure. How does all that blood pressure work, doctor? Does it really have something to do with sugar?"

Sergeant García was very talkative and had the Andalusians' genial accent. Whenever the conversation trailed off and Doctor Da Barca returned to the shelter of his book, he would pick up another thread as if he wanted to prevail over the monotonous jolting of the train. They sat opposite one another, next to the window, while Herbal dozed at a distance, with his rifle in his lap. Alone in the compartment. At one of the stops, when night was already falling, Herbal was woken by the sound of the door. A woman leant in with a child in her arms, holding another by the hand. She wore a headscarf. She said quietly, "Keep going, child, not here."

When he went back to sleep, Herbal heard Doctor Da Barca talking to the nun, Mother Izarne. He was saying to her, "Memories are engrams." "And what are they?" "They're like scars in your head." And then he saw a row of people making scars in his head with the carpenter's chisel. He told most of them that they shouldn't, that they weren't to make scars in his head. Until Marisa appeared, Marisa as a girl, and he said to her, "Yes, make me a scar in my head." And Nan. His head was a piece of alder wood. Nan made a slit and brought his nose closer in order to smell. And then his uncle, the trapper, arrived and stood with his knife in the air, saying, "I'm really sorry, Herbal." And he said, "If you've got to do it, do it, uncle." But then, his head was covered in mud and soot, in Asturias, and a woman was shouting, and the officer was saying, "Shoot, will you, for fuck's sake!" And he was saying, "No, don't make that scar." And then he appeared on a hillside, next to a road, on a moonlit night in August. A young man stood before him in uniform, with a trapper's face, and he was going to ask him why. Why are you making that scar? He remembered the pencil. The carpenter's pencil. The woman with the headscarf said to him, "Keep going, child, not here." And he woke up soaked in sweat, rummaging through his kitbag.

"Hey, corporal! This is your country. Can't you see it's raining? You owe me three night watches!"

And then he muttered, "Some guard! He'd sleep through an air raid."

He found the pencil in the bottom of the bag.

"Hello, Herbal!" the painter said to him. "We've reached Monforte. Here the train divides. I'm off north, to Coruña, and you're heading south. Look after that man!"

"What do you expect me to do?" murmured Herbal. "The relationship's over. I'm not going to San Simón. I've a different posting."

"Look," said the painter. "Look at her!"

And there she was. Her russet hair, the rainbow in her eyes, gradually dispelled the mist on the station platform. The doctor, handcuffed, banged with his two fists on the glass.

"Marisa!"

Sergeant García, who had been so talkative, was struck dumb as if the window were a screen at the cinema.

"Goodbye, Herbal!" said the painter. "I'm off to see how my son is."

"That's my wife!" said the doctor, shaking the sergeant with his handcuffed hands, as excited as if he were announcing the arrival of a queen.

And this is what she was, or rather a queen of seamstresses. "Sergeant García certainly had not been expecting that," Herbal said to Maria da Visitação. "Nor had I. When she leant into the compartment, we did not know whether to fire a salute or to get down on our knees. I pretended not to notice."

Marisa had a picnic basket and a sleeveless dress with a pattern of flowers that clung to her body. It was like the whole of a garden in spring, with bees and everything, entering a cell. The initial contact was inevitable. The wicker basket crackled between the two bodies like a skeleton in the air.

"The embrace knocked me out," Herbal told Maria da Visitação. "The chain of his handcuffs slipped down her back and landed at her waist, above her buttocks."

With the train on the move, Sergeant García decided it was time to take control of the situation. His genial accent became sharp as scissors of steel. They stood apart.

"This is my wife, sergeant," said Doctor Da Barca, as if he were giving water a name.

"We've been on the same train for a thousand years and you never said anything about your wife waiting for you." He exclaimed, gesturing towards the people on the platform, "You might have saved me this circus!"

"He had no idea," Marisa said.

The sergeant gave her a bewildered look, as if she were speaking in French, and took the telegram she offered him. It was signed Mother Izarne from the prison hospital in Porta Coeli and gave her the train times of the transfer.

"I do not wish to appear impolite, doctor," said Sergeant García, "but how do I know you are husband and wife? Your word's not good enough. You must have papers."

"Then I was a coward," Herbal told Maria da Visitação.

"I don't know what came over me. I wanted to say, 'They are, I know they are.' But my voice was swept away."

"I have the papers," replied Marisa with great dignity. And she produced them from the picnic basket.

"The sergeant's attitude changed at once. He was impressed and I'm not surprised," Herbal said. "That woman turned night into day, or *vive-cersa*, as Genghis Khan would say. He took one look around, as if observing procedure, and removed the doctor's handcuffs."

"You may sit down together," he said, pointing to the window. And he kept the basket. He had a healthy appetite.

"Doctor Da Barca took Marisa's hands," said Herbal, before Maria da Visitação could ask him what they were doing. "He was counting her fingers in case she was missing one. She was crying, as if it hurt her to see him."

Suddenly, he stood up and said, "Sergeant, can I interest you in a cigarette?"

They moved to the corridor of the train and smoked not one cigarette, but half a dozen. The train swept alongside the River Miño, tinged with greens and lilacs, and the sergeant and the doctor chatted eagerly as if they were at the bar of the last tavern.

"From the corner where I had been dozing," Herbal said, "I watched her with pity. I felt like throwing the rifle out of the window and embracing her. She was crying and couldn't understand a thing. Nor could I. In a few minutes we would arrive at the station. After that, nothing. Years and years of prison without being able to touch that sewing queen. But there he was, chattering away with the sergeant, like a pair of marketeers. So it went on until we arrived at Vigo station.

"I was surprised when he didn't handcuff him. The sergeant called me to one side, 'Absolute discretion with what we're about to do. If you ever set your tongue wagging, I'll come and find you, even if it means going to hell, and shoot you in the mouth. Understood?'"

"Absolutely, sergeant."

"Well then, take your share. And act normal, for Christ's sake!"

Herbal felt the notes in his hand and put them in his trouser pocket without looking.

"We're both agreed then?"

He looked at him in silence. He had no idea what he was talking about.

"Good. Let's do this couple a favour then. After all, they are married."

Herbal thought that Sergeant García had lost his mind, mesmerized by Doctor Da Barca's hypnotic gaze and persuasive powers. He ought to have foreseen it. Aside from the money he had been given, and it could not be much, what on earth had he told him to cast him under this spell?

"That Daniel is a genius," said the painter in his ear.

"I thought you'd gone," said Herbal in surprise.

"I reconsidered. I couldn't miss this journey!"

"What shall we do then, corporal?" the sergeant asked. "He told me you'd know. He said that you were familiar with Vigo."

The painter punched him on the temple, "The time has come, Herbal. Behave!"

"We can take them to a hotel that's nearby, sir. And let them spend their wedding night at last."

Marisa, unaware of all the scheming going on, quickened her pace across the platform. She wept in silence. To Herbal she was incredibly beautiful, like camellias about to fall. Finally, Da Barca approached her affectionately, but she rejected him, annoyed. "Who are you? You're not Daniel. You're not the man I was waiting for." Until he clasped her by the shoulders, stared into her eyes, embraced her, and whispered in her ear.

"Listen. Don't ask questions. Let yourself go. Tonight will be our wedding night."

Marisa transformed as she began to understand. "Her face turned into that of a bride," Herbal told Maria da Visitação. "They walked peacefully as far as Príncipe Street, as the first lights of evening came on, feigning interest from time to time in the shop windows. Until we arrived at the small hotel nearby. Doctor Da Barca gave a look in the sergeant's direction. The sergeant nodded. And the couple resolutely stepped in."

"Good evening. I am Commander Da Barca," he introduced himself in reception in a severe tone of voice. "Two rooms, if you please, one for me and my wife, and another for the escort. Right. We'll be on our way up. The sergeant will give you the details."

"At your orders, commander. Good night, madam. May you sleep well."

"Good night, Commander Da Barca," Herbal said, standing stiffly to attention. He lowered his head slightly, "Good night, madam."

Sergeant García showed his papers. He said to the receptionist, "Under no circumstances must the commander be disturbed. Please have any messages passed on to me."

"It was a very long night," Herbal told Maria da Visitação. "At least for us it was. I imagine for them it was very short."

"I shouldn't think the turtle-doves will escape," the sergeant said on reaching the room. "But we're not going to run the risk."

So they spent the night taking turns to listen outside the door. "I volunteer for the first shift," Sergeant García had said, winking theatrically at Herbal. "Three times!" he exclaimed when he returned. "Shame there wasn't a hole in the wall."

Had there been a hole in the wall, they would have seen two naked bodies on the bed, the one dressed only in the scarf tied in a knot around her neck that she had once given Daniel in prison.

"I thought I heard someone crying," Herbal told Maria da Visitação. "The wind was up, the sea alive with the sound of accordions.

"Then I heard the bedsprings creaking as well."

Very early, at daybreak, the sergeant gave them a knock at the door. After the long night's vigil he began to feel uneasy about the path they had taken. He paced anxiously around the bed.

"Had the two of you really come to an agreement?"

"I was aware of what was going on," Herbal lied.

"Don't even tell your wife about this," said the sergeant, all of a sudden very serious.

"I don't have a wife," replied Herbal.

"Good. Let's get moving then!"

They kept up the pretence as they left the hotel like a group of poachers. Had the receptionist followed them from the door, he would have seen how Commander Da Barca became a prisoner and was put into handcuffs. In the streets, there was the hung-over light of early morning, the melancholy of cheap rubbish, after a night of accordions in the estuary.

On the quay, a photographer of emigrants offered absentmindedly to take a photograph. The sergeant discouraged him with a rough gesture, "Can't you see he's a prisoner?"

"Are you taking him to San Simón?"

"What do you care?"

"Hardly anyone comes back from there. Let me take their photograph."

"Hardly anyone comes back?" said the doctor suddenly with a bold smile. "A romantic cradle, gentlemen! Which produced the best poem of humanity!"[2]

"Well, it's a graveyard now," muttered the photographer.

"Quick!" the sergeant ordered. "What are you waiting for? Take that photograph, but leave out the chains!"

He embraced her from behind and she covered his arms, so that the handcuffs could not be seen. Merged into one, with the sea in the background. Bags under their eyes from

2 See Appendix II.

their wedding night. Without a great deal of conviction, as a formality, the photographer asked them to smile.

"The last time I saw her," Herbal told Maria da Visitação, "was from the anchorage. We were on the boat. She was standing there, high on the wharf, on her own, leaning against the bollard, her long, russet hair buoyed by the wind.

"He remained upright on the boat, without taking his eyes off the woman on the bollard. I sat in a huddle in the bow. I must be the only Galician who was not born to travel by sea.

"When we reached San Simón, the doctor jumped on to the wharf with a determined air. The sergeant signed a document and handed him over to the guards.

"Before leaving, Doctor Da Barca turned to me. We stared each other in the eyes.

"He said to me,

"'Your problem is not tuberculosis. It has to do with the heart.'"

"You see those on the shore?" said the boatman on the return journey. "They're not washerwomen. They're the prisoners' wives. Sending them food across the sea in Moses baskets."

20

"THEY WERE THE BEST THING THAT EVER HAPPENED to me."

Herbal took the carpenter's pencil and drew a cross on the white of the obituary notice in the newspaper, two coarse lines like the lines a burin makes on a tombstone.

Maria da Visitação read the deceased's name: Daniel Da Barca. Underneath, the name of the wife, Marisa Mallo, the son, daughter, and a long trail of grandchildren.

At the top, on the right, by way of an epitaph, a poem by Antero de Quental. Maria da Visitação read it out slowly in her Portuguese with a Creole accent.

> But if I stop for a moment, succeed
> in closing my eyes, I can feel them near me
> Once more, those that I loved living with me . . .

"Herbal, you're going to spoil the girl for me with all that literature!"

Manila, who had just come down from the first floor, was

pouring herself a coffee at the bar. Today she seemed in a good mood.

"I only ever knew one man who could recite poems. And he was a priest! They were beautiful poems that talked about blackbirds and love."

"You and a priest poet?" said Herbal mockingly. "A fine couple, indeed."

"He was a charming man. A gentleman, and not like others in a cassock. Don Faustino. According to him, God had to be a woman. Whenever he went out for the night wearing plain clothes, he'd say, 'Now, to be sure, Christ himself wouldn't recognize me!' A bit naive. His life was made impossible for him."

She swallowed the coffee in one gulp, "Right, you can think about finishing the conversation. We open in half an hour."

"I never saw them again," Herbal told Maria da Visitação. "I found out Marisa had given birth to a boy, when he was still on San Simón. The child from their wedding night! Doctor Da Barca was released in the mid-fifties. After that they left for America. And I heard nothing more about them. I didn't even know they had returned."

Herbal did a conjuring trick with the carpenter's pencil. He managed it as if it were a finger on the loose.

"My life changed pretty soon afterwards. Having handed over the prisoner on San Simón, I went back to Coruña, where I discovered that my sister was very ill. In the head, I mean. I shot Zalito Puga. To be honest, I shot him three times. That's what let me down. I had planned it all carefully. I was going to allege that a bullet had fired off as I was cleaning the gun. That kind of thing happened a lot in those days. But I lost control at the last moment and fired at him three times. So I was expelled from the corps and ended up in prison. There I met Manila's brother. And then I met her, when she came visiting. I had no-one any more. She was my only window on to the world. When they let me out, she said to me, 'I'm fed up of pimps. I need a man who's not afraid.'

"And here I am."

"And what happened to the painter?" Maria da Visitação asked.

"He came to see me once in prison. A day of anguish, when I was short of breath. The deceased spoke to me and the breathlessness went away. He said to me, 'You know something? I found my son. He spends his time painting mothers and their newborn babies.'

"'That's a good sign,' I said to him. 'It signifies hope.'

"'Very good, Herbal. Now you know something about painting.'"

"And didn't he come back?"

"No, he never came back," Herbal lied. "As Doctor Da Barca would have said, he disappeared into eternal indifference."

Maria da Visitação had tears in her eyes. She had learnt to hold back the tears, but not to control her emotions.

"Look, the camellias glisten after the rain," the painter said in Herbal's ear. "Give her the pencil! Give it to the dark-haired girl!"

"Here, a present," he said, holding out the carpenter's pencil.

"But . . . "

"Take it, please."

Manila clapped her hands in the air as usual and opened the door to the club. There was one client waiting.

"He was here the other day," said Herbal in a changed voice. The guard's voice, "You've work, girl!"

"He's grown attached," she said ironically. "He told me he was a journalist. He's a bit depressed."

"A depressed journalist?" The voice had turned to one of disgust, "Watch out. Make sure he pays before he goes to bed."

"Where are you off to?" Manila asked him in surprise.

"I'm going outside a while. For a breath of fresh air."

"Wrap up warm!"

"I'll only be a minute."

Herbal leant against the hinge of the door. In the wet and windy night, the neon sign with its Valkyrian figure flickered with sad obscenity. The dog in the scrapyard barked at the procession of headlights, a burin's litany in the dark. Herbal noticed the sense of breathlessness and longed for a gust of wind to sweep through him. On the sand track leading to the road, he saw her coming at last. Death with her white shoes. Instinctively, he felt for the carpenter's pencil. "Come on, bitch, I've nothing now!" Why was she so quiet? Why did she not curse that slut, Life, and the smiling accordionist who had taken her?

"Come inside, Herbal!" Manila said, wrapping him in her black lace shawl. "What are you doing out here on your own like a dog?"

"Phantom pain," he muttered under his breath.

"What was that, Herbal?"

"Nothing."

AUTHOR'S NOTE

Out of consideration for those who inspired me to write this story,
I should point out that it is a work of fiction, and in no way biograph-
ical. All of the characters, except for those who are mentioned by
name in the scene from the old prison of Santiago, are the fruit of
invention. There is no real correspondence to be found. That they
should belong to what Doctor Nóvoa Santos called the "overworld"
is quite another matter.

APPENDIX I

ROSALÍA DE CASTRO'S POEM "JUSTICE BY THE HAND" (CHAPTER 6)

The ones in the town that are viewed with respect
Stole all of the purity I once possessed,
They covered in litter my own Sunday best,
The clothes I was wearing they tore into shreds.

Where I had been living no stone was there left,
No hearth and no shelter, I turned and I fled.
In fields with the hares in the open I slept.
My children . . . my angels! . . . for whom my heart wept
Put up with such hunger they died, they were dead!

My honour was broken, my life at an end,
Of brambles and gorse was the bed they had made,
And meanwhile the villains of damnable name
At ease amid roses were taking their rest.

"O judges, please save me!" I cried . . . but in vain!
They laughed at me, justice knew not what I meant.
"Good God, won't you help me?" I cried, I cried yet . . .
Good God was so high that he missed what I said.

So then like a she-wolf that suffers in pain,
I leapt for the sickle and left in a rage,
I circled round slowly . . . No grass heard my step!
The moon clouded over, and on a soft bed
The beast with its partners had yet to awake.

I looked at them calmly, my arms were outstretched,
In one, one fell swoop! their lives there I reft.
And next to my victims I sat down content,
At ease as I waited for morning to break.

And then . . . it was then that our justice was kept:
On them, mine; the laws on the hand they had met.

(Rosalía de Castro, *Follas novas* (1880), II.xxv;
translated by Jonathan Dunne)

"THE BEST POEM OF HUMANITY" (CHAPTER 19),
BY THE 13th-CENTURY GALICIAN-PORTUGUESE
TROUBADOUR POET MENDINHO

At Saint Simon's chapel I took my seat
and was caught by the waves, how tall they seem.
I was waiting for my friend! Will he come?

At the chapel before the altar-stone
I was caught by the waves, they seem to grow.
I was waiting for my friend! Will he come?

And was caught by the waves, how tall they seem,
I have no boatman to row for me.
I was waiting for my friend! Will he come?

And was caught by the waves, the sea below,
I have no boatman, nor know how to row.
I was waiting for my friend! Will he come?

I have no boatman to row for me,
fair maid I shall die on the open sea.
I was waiting for my friend! Will he come?

I have no boatman, nor know how to row,
fair maid I shall die on the sea below.
I was waiting for my friend! Will he come?

(Mendinho in Giuseppe Tavani,
A poesía lírica galego-portuguesa
(3rd edition, 1991), p. 132;
translated by Jonathan Dunne)